SECRET OBSESSION

JILL SANDERS

GRAYTON

To my Frassistant, Amelia

Thanks, girl,
for being so freaking amazeballs.

SUMMARY

Being the son of the famous Senator Rhodes thrust Blake into the limelight from a very young age. After surviving a kidnapping when he was eight years old, he knew that he wanted to follow his father into the political arena. But bumping into a beautiful starlet at a charity event turns his life upside down, all because of a stolen kiss.

Robin is at the top of her career. So it's only natural that she wants to enjoy her success. But with that success come the standard creeps and stalkers. After rumors of a relationship between her and a young congressmen go public, things take a much darker turn.

PROLOGUE

Blake tried not to make a sound as he cried in the darkness. He'd peed himself some time ago and now his wet pants were cold, making him shiver. He'd been knocked out for a while and had lost track of time, so he wasn't even sure it was still the same day.

The last thing he remembered was his father's driver picking him up from school. By the time he realized it wasn't Carl, the normal driver, and that another man was sitting in the back of the limo with him, it was too late for him to scream. Then everything had gone dark. He had no idea where they'd taken him since they'd blindfolded and gagged him.

Now, his eight-year-old body was no match for four grown men. When he'd cried out, he'd been kicked in the gut, which had caused him to cry even more.

"Shut up, kid," someone had said in a deep voice. But he hadn't listened. He'd just kept crying.

He'd fallen asleep crying and woke when he was picked up, carried, and then tossed on a hard floor.

The gag had been removed, and he cried out. When he

noticed that the blindfold had been removed as well, he looked around and saw that he was in a very dark room. Alone.

He thought about his parents, his older sister. Of how he would probably never see them again. He'd never get to go to school again. He cried for all of the things that he'd miss. His home, his family, and his friends. He'd dreamed of becoming a superhero. How was he going to do that now if he couldn't even save himself?

After that, he was left alone for a long time and fell asleep again.

The next time he woke, four men were standing over him, yelling at one another. He thought to sneak away since they weren't paying attention to him, but they kept pointing at him and yelling.

He didn't understand everything they were saying, but two of them weren't happy they weren't asking for more money.

He'd watched a movie with his older sister, Ann, where someone had been kidnapped and the girl's parents had paid a ransom. Were these men wanting his father to pay to have him released?

He knew without a doubt that his father would pay whatever the men wanted. After all, he was Senator Kenneth Rhodes, one of the most powerful men in the world. Or so Blake thought. That was, until the four men stood over him.

The leader was a short, balding man that the others called Miles. Blake jumped when he slammed his gun down on the table that they'd put him on and told everyone to shut up.

Instantly, the room grew silent. Miles picked up a cell

phone from the table and dialed a number as he walked towards the back of the house.

Blake was the only one in the room that noticed a fifth man appear from the shadows in a full GI Joe commando outfit. Blake's eyes were glued to him as he moved silently and started picking off each of the three remaining men. The man rushed behind the first bad guy and snapped his neck before the other two could respond. Blake listened for the sound he'd heard in the movies, but instead of a bone-crushing sound, he heard the man's breath whoosh out quietly.

The second bad guy went down as quietly with a quick punch to the throat. The third man got a knife in his throat and went down in the pile.

Miles continued to talk on the phone as GI Joe guy picked up the gun he'd set down on the table and pointed it at the back of Miles's head.

"Move and you're dead, just like your buddies," GI Joe said. Blake couldn't have imagined a cooler line. Just like in the movies. Miles tensed as he held the phone up to his ear.

Blake rolled slightly on the table to see what would happen next.

"Commander here, the room is secure," GI Joe said to the room as Miles slowly dropped the phone to the floor in shock.

Blake gasped slightly. GI Joe had come to save him. See, he knew his dad would do anything to get Blake back. Even hire GI Joe.

Then Blake watched in horror as Miles spun around and hit GI Joe on the side of his ear. GI Joe didn't even flitch. He chuckled as he wiped a trickle of blood from his ear.

"You shouldn't have done that," GI Joe said as he used the butt of his gun to make a dent in the man's forehead.

Once Miles was on the floor in a heap of unconscious bad guy, the man turned towards Blake.

"Are you a GI Joe?" Blake asked him, totally forgetting about the past twenty-some hours of fear and hell. He was meeting his hero. Scratch that—his hero was rescuing him. The past few moments had been better than any he'd ever imagined. Better than any video game or movie he'd ever seen.

"Sure, kid," GI Joe said as he walked towards him. "Let's get you home to your dad." The man lifted Blake from the table and carried him out into the night.

He couldn't remember the car ride home, except that he kept asking questions of GI Joe, whose real name was Ethan Knight, a much cooler name than GI Joe, at least in Blake's mind.

The man personally handed Blake over to his father and mother. That would have been cool, except his mother made a mess and cried on him and hugged him so tight, Blake couldn't say goodbye or thank you to Ethan.

That night Blake's entire world changed. He was no longer an eight-year-old ready to conquer the world. Instead, he was a boy who knew that bad guys were just around the corner and that heroes did exist.

He spent years in counseling that he believed at first that he didn't need or want. He had no scars from the time, other than the ones on the inside. Years later, he would be thankful for those hours and the help he'd received. From that night on, Blake Rhodes didn't trust easily.

CHAPTER ONE

T wenty years later...

Robin Stein slid on the pale-colored lipstick and glanced at her reflection one more time in the small compact before stuffing it into the clutch that matched her soft cream dress perfectly.

Tonight, she was wearing Rubio's latest diamond-encrusted nude cream design. Rubio was one of her go-to designers for events like this. Rubio's designs were a little less... Hollywood.

Since this event, a charity ball, coincided with her shooting schedule, her agent Amanda Hughes had arranged for a ticket and had set up the gown, jewelry, hair, and makeup that went along with all her very public events.

Robin liked to be pampered, but she had been looking forward to a night in. She had planned on ordering the largest steak the Ritz Carlton could give her from room service and pig out in her deluxe suite.

Instead, the moment filming had finished for the day, she'd let Carlos and Carmen, the husband-and-wife team that took care of her hair and makeup, into her suite.

For the next two hours, she'd looked over her lines for the following shoot as they did their thing and got her ready.

She loved acting. From the moment she'd stepped onto the stage at age five after winning her very first lead in the *Christmas Carol* play at her school, she'd known what she wanted to do for the rest of her life. Sure, at times it was hard work. The hours were long during the shooting, but there was never a dull moment. When she had downtime, she read, always on the lookout for her next project. Or she scoured magazines, looking for her next look or hairstyle, or a worthy cause to get behind.

Tonight's event was for one of her favorite causes, and Amanda had reminded her to take a couple of pics for her to post on social media to highlight the foundation. Robin opted for a picture of her standing out on the balcony of her suite with the Colonne Vendôme in the background.

The cream of her dress contrasted nicely with the green color of the Colonne Vendôme. As she walked down the marble staircase to get into her waiting limo, Carmen took a few more shots of her. She sent the best to Amanda on the ride to the Musée de l'Homme, or the Museum of Mankind, where the party would be hosted. The museum sat directly across the Seine River from the Eiffel Tower.

She'd spent three whole days enjoying all of the local museums, including the Louvre and the Homme, on her first trip to Paris almost eight years ago. Since that trip, she'd been back to the city of love more than a dozen times.

She loved Paris, she did, but she'd been in the city for over two months now shooting her latest movie, *It Takes Two*. She had less than a month to go in filming, and then she could take a break before the big push for the release started.

This time, she was thinking of a trip to Barbados. Or maybe she'd stay in Europe and head to Italy?

When the limo slowed, she pasted on her smile, checked her cleavage, since the dress hung a little lower than she liked, and stepped out to the many flashes from the paparazzi.

Being Robin Stein didn't come as naturally as it used to. She used to be a long-legged quirky teenage girl. That had gained her the attention and eyes of television producer Jeff Hartland. For three years, Robin had been quirky teenager Molly McBride in the hit show *Raising Molly*.

She'd moved from television to film shortly after the show had ended with Molly going off to college, something Robin hadn't done herself, at least not right away and then only online classes.

Instead, she'd gotten her first big movie role as Kim Lost, a sidekick to the superhero in a movie called *Magnanimous*.

For the next few years, she had played alongside some of the best actors and actresses in three more movies, including one where she had played opposite the lead as the villain. Finally, after the first couple of movies, she'd earned her first lead role.

It Takes Two was the third movie she was lead in and her first romantic comedy. She had fallen in love with the book the moment she'd picked a copy up at the airport. Amanda had hunted down the producers and the author and requested to audition for the lead in the upcoming movie.

She'd been happily surprised when she'd gotten the role. It had meant spending more time overseas and since she had been dealing with... issues in California, she'd needed a reason to stay out of the States.

Walking into a party alone had never really been an issue for her before. Now, however, she realized that she was the lone actress in a very political arena. There were so many politicians and activists in the room that she started believing it was a mistake for her to be there.

Tonight's charity event was a fundraiser for Global Climate Awareness. GCA was raising funds for their newest project, which would pull plastics out of the world's oceans and recycle it.

Robin was passionate about the project and had been following GCA's progress around the globe so far. Still, she had hoped that there would be more actors and actresses in attendance. Instead, the room was filled with diplomats and politicians, none of whom she had anything in common with.

She'd strolled around the room once already and was thinking of sneaking out early. She was already on her second glass of champagne when she bumped into the back of a man in a black Armani suit. The first thing she noticed about him was his piercing blue eyes. The next was that he was easily the sexiest man in the room. Trust her, she'd been on the lookout for someone to flirt with.

"Sorry," the man said as he took her arm gently so that she didn't topple of the three-inch spiky heels that matched her dress.

"No, that was my fault. I wasn't watching where I was going," she replied, not sure if she should tell him she'd been preoccupied with trying to find the door to leave. Since walking in, she'd heard lots of people talk about her, but so far no one had approached and struck up a conversation.

The man smiled, and her heart skipped a beat. "So,

what is Robin Stein doing at a GCA event?" he asked her with a smile.

She shifted her weight and took a sip of her champagne. "Can't actresses be involved in saving the planet?"

His smile doubled, and she thought he looked very familiar. "Not the actors and actresses I know..." He shook his head. "Other than the handful that are considered major activists." The man was flirting with her, and she found it utterly delightful. He was a sexy package complete with looks, charm, and mystery. Part of her wished to keep flirting without knowing who he was. The way he moved and talked hinted that he came from money.

She'd known many people who had come into money by one means or another. They usually stood out from the ones who'd had wealth their entire lives.

Not that she had been raised with a silver spoon in her mouth, but she was a damn good actress and could easily fake it around the right people. The ones she needed to influence.

"You must not know a lot of actors," she teased.

"Not the right ones." He held out his hand for her. "Blake Rhodes."

"Robin." She took his hand, but then stilled when his name struck her, and it dawned on her who he was. "Senator Rhodes?" She blinked and suddenly she knew exactly where she'd seen the man before. He was currently the youngest senator in the States. He'd been dubbed the sexiest man alive last year and it was obvious why now that she was face-to-face with the man. He oozed sex appeal.

"Guilty," he replied.

"I hadn't heard you were in Paris or that you'd be attending this event," she said. In truth, she hadn't even had time to research who was attending tonight's event.

"I hadn't planned on it. I just arrived in Paris earlier today for another meeting." He shrugged slightly. "I decided to get out for the night. Besides, it's a worthy cause. I've been following the project for a while now." His smile grew as he lowered his voice. "I've been following your career as well. You're taking Hollywood by storm, or so the media says."

She smiled. "Do you believe everything the media writes?"

He laughed. "Hell no."

She remembered there had been some rumors in the tabloids about his personal life not too long ago.

"Good." She smiled. "Neither do I." She saw him relax slightly as she ran her eyes up and down his suit. "Sexiest man alive?" She shook her head in disbelief and had him laughing.

"Right." He rolled his eyes. His hand came out and touched her elbow to guide her away from a waiter that was about to knock his tray into her shoulder.

In the last few moments that she'd been talking with him, the room had filled with even more guests. Now the place was extremely crowded and had grown loud as everyone chatted and laughed. There was a band playing somewhere in the massive building, and music echoed in the hall.

"How about some air?" He nodded towards glass doors.

Nodding, she followed him through the crowd, enjoying the feel of his hand on her lower back.

She was enjoying flirting with him, watching his eyes heat as she felt her own body warm. When was the last time she'd felt such an instant pull of attraction? When was the last time she'd acted on such a feeling? Never, if she was being honest with herself.

Sure, she had taken plenty of lovers, but only after weeks or, in a few cases, months of dating. After a few scares, she'd learned to be more cautious about who she was with. Especially after she'd earned her Hollywood star.

The moment she'd stepped into the stage lights, men had come out of the woodwork to pursue, stalk, or just plain harass her. Not to mention all the hate that had come along with the fame.

More than once, she had been called out for being either too thin, too fat, too short, too tall, too blonde, too young, too old—the list went on. For the first year, she'd cried or had grown angry over each article. Then, one day, things had just clicked.

She'd stopped caring what the haters were saying and had started listening to her own body, her own feelings. Only after that had she'd started having fun and enjoying her job.

"This is much better," he said once they were outside and had stepped onto the Palais de Chaillot.

They started strolling across the courtyard, the Eiffel Tower directly across from them. At this time of night, the lights had yet to flicker on. She knew that within the hour the anticipated light show would be watched all over the city.

The museum had been cleared of all tours and tourists for the special event. However, here in the courtyard, some tourists were enjoying the large glass structure. Still, it was relatively dark, and Robin didn't think anyone would recognize them. She draped her hand through his arm, and they strolled towards the lighted tower.

"This city never ceases to amaze, does it?" He turned slightly towards her.

"No." She smiled and, instead of looking at the scenery,

she ran her eyes over him again. "It must be difficult being the youngest senator. The young pup among all the old dogs?"

He nodded. "I was born for it."

"That's right, your father..." Then she remembered hearing the story about his childhood. How he'd been kidnapped when he was eight.

"Yeah, there it is." He nodded. "That look everyone gets when they remember my story." Blake sighed. "Even you're not a good enough actress to hide it."

"Sorry. I guess I should have warmed up first," she teased and enjoyed seeing his smile return.

"Nice recovery." He leaned closer to her. "So, if my memory serves me, you were raised in Colorado?"

"Yes, we moved to California when I was fifteen. I got my first acting job shortly after." She smiled.

"You have a younger sister?" he asked.

"Claire," she supplied. "She's an aspiring clothing designer," she said proudly. "I wear a lot of her designs normally." She glanced down at the borrowed gown.

"This?" he asked, running his finger over the lace covering her shoulder.

She shook her head. "No, this is borrowed for tonight," she admitted. "You?" She mimicked his move and ran a finger over the lapel of his jacket.

"Mine." He chuckled. "In my line of work, it pays to always pack for black tie events."

"Right." She took a step closer to him, enjoying the musky scent of his cologne. "Are you in Paris for just one night?" she asked him, imagining what it would be like to have those lips covering her own.

"A few weeks," he answered. "You?"

"There is less than a month left in filming," she answered as he moved a step closer to her.

She watched his eyebrows arch upwards. "Another movie? I thought you just finished filming the one in Canada?"

"A few months back." She shrugged. "I like to keep busy."

"Where is home?" he asked.

She remembered something about him being from the Atlanta area.

"Right now, Santa Barbara." She thought about the apartment she had spent less than a month in this year. "You?"

"I have a home in Atlanta, just a few miles from my childhood home." He looked over as the sun slipped even lower, making the sky turn a rainbow of cotton candy colors.

"It's beautiful," she said, watching the sky.

"Yes," he said, and she realized he was still looking at her. Turning back to him, she took a step closer. "I want to kiss you." His eyes moved to her lips.

"What's stopping you?" she asked, moving even closer.

He flashed a smile as his hands moved up to her waist while he closed the rest of the distance. The moment their bodies bumped, her breath caught in her lungs. The scent of him filled her senses as he dipped his head towards hers.

When his lips brushed over hers, she could have sworn time stood still. Her entire body tingled seconds before it heated and started to vibrate with instant want.

She had never experienced anything like it before. Her brain stopped functioning as he slanted his lips over hers. The slight roughness of his beard brushing against her chin while his soft lips parted her own was something she'd never expected to enjoy so much. He tasted like champagne so sweet she had to have more.

At first, she didn't understand what the flashes were, since she'd closed her eyes on a moan when he'd taken the kiss deeper, but then she'd felt him stiffen and pull away.

Blinking, she watched as Blake took a step-in front of her, shielding her body from the onslaught of bright lights. Then she realized they'd been found. Even worse, they'd been photographed in what she could only describe as the most tender moment of her life.

CHAPTER TWO

Blake was used to being stalked by the press. But never to this level. Being followed and photographed in a private moment, or what should have been a private moment, just pissed him off.

Still, he did his best to get Robin back into the event without seeming too overbearing. The last thing he wanted was to be labeled aggressive towards the press. In his line of work, he'd learned that he couldn't be conceived as a pushover but also couldn't appear too tyrannical.

"That was fun," he said the moment they stepped back into the hallway of the museum.

"I'm sorry," Robin said, turning towards him. The night air had turned her cheeks a brighter shade of pink. Her eyes were laughing at him and her lips... He had to avoid looking there, or the sight of the plump pinkness would only make him want to kiss her again.

"For?" he asked, realizing he was still holding her hand. He had no intention of letting it go.

She was silent for a moment and then chuckled. "You know what? Nothing. I'm not sorry. Normally, I have to explain to... someone I'm with about being stalked." She tilted her head slightly and smiled. "But something tells me you understand."

He chuckled. "I've been in the press for a very long time."

She nodded. "What do you say we get out of here? Find someplace... private?"

His entire body heated and jumped at her suggestion. There was nothing he wanted more than to have an amazing affair with Robin Stein in the city of love.

But then he thought about how much that one kiss and the past hour of conversation with her had meant to him, and he knew that a one-night stand with her wouldn't satisfy his thirst to spend more time with such an amazing person. He thought of the perfect private place where they could go and be alone.

"I have the perfect place to go." He started walking towards the door, then stopped. "Do you need to check in with..." He motioned towards the party.

"Nope, all good." She tugged his arm, pulling him towards the door.

They made their way into the foyer and waited until they were signaled that their limo had arrived. The moment they stepped out front, they were once again surrounded by flashes as they darted for the limo.

He initially tried to shield her but when he heard several of the cameramen calling her name, he remembered that she was probably as used to the attention as he was. If not more so.

"And the fun continues," he said when they were tucked safely in the limo.

Instead of answering, she pulled closer to him and plastered her body against his. He had a difficult time remembering he was trying to play the gentlemen.

"Where shall we go?" she asked almost purring. "My place or yours?"

"I was thinking…" He dipped his head down to brush his lips over hers and allowed himself a moment to enjoy the taste of her. The feel of her against him. Her lips were soft, and she tasted like cinnamon and nectar. "That we'd go someplace more private."

He watched her eyebrows rise slightly. "Where in Paris is there someplace more private than a hotel room?"

He smiled. "You'll just have to wait and see." He pulled out his cell phone and sent a text message to the driver.

"Oh, we're in your limo." she said, as she looked around. "They all look alike back here."

"Is that a problem?"

"No." She pulled out her phone and sent a text. "I just need to tell Phillip he can have the rest of the evening off."

"Your driver?" he asked, putting his phone in his pocket as the limo headed out of the city.

"Yes," she answered. She tucked her phone back into her purse. "Now, where were we?" She tossed her purse onto the seat next to them and wrapped her arms around his shoulders.

"Would you think me a cad if I told you I didn't remember?" he asked playfully.

She chuckled. "Your reputation precedes you, Senator Rhodes. I've read a few articles from several of your exes, and they all agree that you are no cad."

"Oh?" he said, feeling his stomach lurch. "What else have you heard?"

Her smile grew. "That you have a few dark shadows in your closet, but nothing too iniquitous."

He relaxed and started running his hands over her dress. It was the first time he could remember being with someone as educated as he was. He remembered reading an article about her history. How she'd spent the last few years not only making movies but getting her degree while she was at it. For her, education had been as much a priority as working. She'd given up most of her personal time for her classes.

"It's nice," he said between kisses.

"Hm?" she asked, pulling back and looking up into his eyes.

He'd meant to think his thoughts to himself, but now he sighed. "Being with someone who knows what iniquitous means."

There was a slight pause and then she laughed. "So the rumors about your last two girlfriends are true then?" He frowned slightly. "Oh, come on." She shifted away slightly. "You've dated models and"—she tilted her head slightly—"backup dancers. There was bound to be some intelligence there."

"So have you, or so I've read." He smiled. "There was some, but none to, shall I say, the level that I've experienced from you so far." He pulled her back towards him.

"Flattery will get you everywhere," she purred, then she glanced out the dark windows. "Where are we going?"

"I'm staying just outside of town. There's plenty to do at the château, and I thought we'd have a better time going for a walk minus the paparazzi."

Her eyes grew large and she gasped. "Château de Ferrières? You're taking me to Château de Ferrières? Your family's private château?"

"Unless you object?" he asked, seeing her excitement.

"No, no objections." She shifted in her seat and glanced

out the dark windows, as if she could already see the massive structure. "I do wish it was daytime. I'd love to see all of it."

"Then you'll have to come back tomorrow," he suggested. "It's only a twenty-minute drive."

"Or…" she turned back to him with a smile. "I could always stay until the sun comes up."

He chuckled. "That's another option. There are plenty of spare rooms."

She touched the lapel of his jacket. "Afraid I'll hog the covers?"

Smiling, he shook his head. "I'm trying very hard to be a gentleman."

"I'd heard that about you." She brushed her lips across his jawline. "You don't have to be a gentleman on my account. I think we're both adult enough to know that we want one another."

He nodded, swallowing the lump in his throat. "I didn't bring you out here to force your hand," he said honestly.

"I had already made up my mind." She smiled as she kissed him again, and she began tugging his dinner jacket off his shoulders. He allowed her to undress him, pulling off his jacket and tie, and unbuttoning his shirt. He explored only the bare skin exposed by her long-sleeved dress.

It was enough, for now, to run his hands over the lace that was tight against her skin. To hike the long material of the skirt up and run his hands over the softness of her legs, which were lying over his legs.

When she reached for the zipper of his pants, he gripped her hand, stopping her as the limo slowed and turned into the final curve.

"We're here." He nodded towards the windows.

It took her a moment to register his words. Then she

gasped and leaned towards the window. "Wow, it's even more beautiful than the pictures."

He remembered the first time he'd seen Château de Ferrières. He'd been ten. His mother, Coleen, had nagged his father after his kidnapping to purchase a place overseas where they could escape and have some quality family time.

His father, being the kind of man who didn't do anything small, had purchased the château. For the next ten years, the family had spent more than three months in the nineteenth-century stone château.

As a kid, he'd loved exploring the massive place. Part of it had been blocked off specifically for the family's private use, while other parts were rented out for major events such as weddings. But his mother and father made sure that never happened when the family was in residence.

The place was as much home to him as his childhood home and his new residence a few miles outside of Atlanta.

"Would you like a tour or to take a walk in the gardens?" he asked as he helped her out of the limo. He'd rebuttoned his shirt but had left his tie and jacket off since it was warm enough.

"I'd love both," she said. She turned into his arms. "Later." She lowered her voice. "For now, I'm too eager to see if they photoshopped the six-pack that was on full display in those vacation pictures someone snapped of you on the beach."

He chuckled. "You'd be surprised how many times I've been asked that." He took her hand and walked through the massive glass and iron doors. Just inside were two marble staircases. She'd seen so many images of them that she felt like she'd been there before. As they climbed to the main floor, he pointed out some of the paintings and statues.

Then they stepped into the two-story foyer, which was one of the most photographed rooms in the château.

"I bet you had a blast living here when you were a kid." She ran her fingers over the banister and stopped on the top stair. "Did you ever..." She motioned to the railing.

He laughed. "Several times." He leaned towards her. "Tempted?"

She bit her bottom lip and then laughed. "Not in this dress." She motioned to her evening gown.

"Later then." He took her hand again and walked towards another set of marble staircases. "The family's rooms are on the top floor in the east wing. The west wing, which overlooks the larger garden and lake, are saved for event rentals."

"Are there any events scheduled during your stay?" she asked.

"No, I had the next two weeks blacked out."

"Right. For some reason I thought you'd be staying in the city. I'd forgotten your family owned this place until you mentioned it." She stopped at the railing and took one last look at the open staircase before stepping into the private hallway.

The moment they stepped into his room, she pushed him against the heavy wood door and plastered her body against his while her hands pushed his clothing from him.

"Easy," he warned, only to lose his control when she scraped her teeth against his jaw.

"We can take it easy later," she said, her eyes locked with his. "For now, let's do fast." She smiled.

"I can do fast." He chuckled and reached for the zipper on the back of her dress. "But since I know this is a loaner, what do you say we get you out of it without tearing it?"

She blinked her eyes a few times and then sighed.

"You're right." She turned to face away from him as he slowly unzipped the fragile material.

"Wow, later we're going to talk about this room." She pushed her long hair to the side, giving him better access.

He wanted to go slow, to enjoy the soft perfect skin that was exposed as the material slipped from her shoulders. She was wearing nude undergarments, the kind all the women he'd been with wore under fancy attire. Only when the dress hit the floor did he notice it wasn't exactly like what he was used to.

"Garter belts?" he asked, running a finger over her thighs as she took the dress from his hands.

"Yes," she answered as she glanced over her shoulder at him. "Can I hang this?"

Since his mouth had gone dry, he motioned to his walk-in closet, where he kept an entire wardrobe of clothes on hand so he didn't have to carry luggage each time he visited.

She opened the door and turned on the light, and let out a little whistle.

"You don't live here full time, do you?" she called out from inside the closet.

"No. I just keep my closet stocked for all occasions when I'm here," he answered when she stepped back out into his rooms.

He met her halfway across the room. In the next seconds, his shirt and pants hit the ground. Her hands ran over his chest and arms as he focused on her mouth, enjoying her taste.

"Robin." Her name came out as a warning when she rubbed her fingers over his hardness.

"I did say I wanted speed," she teased.

He took a deep breath, and the scent of her removed the last threads of his control. He tried not to be too rough as he pulled, nudged, and tore the nude-colored lace from her body. She moaned with pleasure when he cupped her breasts, covered one with his mouth, and sucked her nipple into his mouth.

Her fingers dug into his hair, scraped his neck and jaw as she fought for him to move faster.

When he tore her panties aside and plunged his fingers into her, she cried out his name and arched into him.

"Blake, now. I need..." She dropped off on a moan when his fingers moved deeper into her.

He felt her convulse, felt her slickness, and growled in a pure primal moment. He swung her up into his arms and gently laid her almost limp body on the bed.

CHAPTER THREE

R obin watched Blake take a condom from his nightstand and quickly sheath himself. He removed his boxer briefs before lying beside her.

Smiling, she pulled him down to her and moaned with pleasure when he slid slowly into her.

"I know you wanted speed," he said into her hair, "but for this part, I'd like to take my time."

Her smile doubled. "You read my mind." She sighed and held onto him as he kissed her and built her back up. His hands moved over her as if he knew just where she wanted to be touched—needed to be touched.

She'd had a handful of lovers in her lifetime, but none had been this experienced in what she wanted during their first time together. My god, he'd made her come moments after he'd touched her.

Already, she could feel herself slipping towards the edge again. His mouth and tongue covered hers, then slid lower to suck her nipple in as his hands, oh god, his hands.

She felt her entire body tense once more as his name slipped from her lips.

"Robin." Blake's deep voice woke her from the afterglow.

"Hmm," she said, realizing he was lying beside her, his arms wrapped around her.

"I'm going to get some water. Would you like anything?" he asked her.

She smiled and snuggled further into him. "Water is good."

She cracked her eyes open and watched him crawl out of the massive bed and walk naked across the wood floors towards a small bar area. His back was as impressive as his front. He was all lean, long, toned muscles with perfect tanned skin. She'd noticed a tattoo on his left pec, but she'd been too preoccupied to recognize the symbol.

Now, as he walked back towards her with a glass of water, her eyes scanned his chest.

He sat beside her, and she took the glass from him. Reaching up, she traced the symbol.

"Military?" she asked, trying to place it.

He glanced down and then back at her and laughed. "Something like that." He relaxed as his eyes moved down to the small tattoo just above her left hips. His hand reached out and he traced the outline of the knife with the snake wrapped around it with his finger.

"A warning?" he asked her.

"Something like that," she answered, not wanting to go into the symbolism at the moment.

"Later?" he asked, taking the half-empty glass from her.

"Yes." She smiled and pulled him back onto the bed.

This time, as they moved together, she paid very close attention to his needs. She'd been too wrapped up in her pleasure earlier.

"Let go," he urged her. "When you're pleased, I get my pleasure," he said next to her ear.

It was all the encouragement she needed. She shifted and focused on what he was doing to her body. Instantly, she felt herself building up once more.

"Yes," he encouraged her. "That's it." He kissed her until she felt herself slip gently off the massive cliff that was her orgasm. This time, however, she felt Blake join her. His body tensed above her own and then moments later, he shifted to lie beside her.

"I don't want to move," she said with a sigh.

"Then don't," he said next to her ear.

"Hm, I have to be back in the city in the morning. Filming starts pretty early." She inwardly groaned.

"You could get a few hours of rest first. Then I'll drive you back to your hotel myself," he suggested.

She thought about letting herself fall asleep in his arms. Taking the time to enjoy the feeling of sleeping next to the man who had just pleased her three times in the past hour. Sighing, she laid her head on his chest. "A few hours." She closed her eyes.

"Alexa, set an alarm for three hours," Blake said just as she drifted off.

The alarm woke them both, and she was far more refreshed than she would have thought she'd be. Stretching, she leaned up and kissed Blake just before he rolled out of bed.

"How about a shower first?" he asked, his eyes running over her.

"I would love a shower." She followed him into the large, attached bathroom. "You wouldn't happen to have a change of clothes somewhere?" she asked.

"My sister's room is just through there." He motioned to the door directly through the bathroom.

"Sister…" She thought for a moment, trying to remember the logistics of his family.

"Ann and Ethan, her husband, visit at least twice a year with their three kids," he said, turning on the shower. "She's bound to have something in there that will fit you."

He pulled her under the warm spray. "Ahh, so it's not true what they say about these old castles and their plumbing."

He chuckled. "My mother and I spent an entire summer remodeling these rooms."

She glanced up at him in surprise. "You did?"

He rubbed shampoo through her long hair, and she practically purred at the touch.

"Yeah, I was ten and was still struggling a bit," he said, a slight strain in his tone.

"Because of your kidnapping?" she asked, feeling relaxed in his hands. He tensed for a moment, but then answered after he sighed.

"Yeah. My mother figured that if I was busy working, I wouldn't have time to think about what had happened to me."

"Did it work?" she asked, glancing up at him.

He smiled. "Yeah, I still use the method. It's why I built my place outside of Atlanta."

"You built your home? Yourself?" she asked. She'd seen several pictures of his massive barndominium. The place was picturesque.

"Yup. Turning an old barn into a home was nothing compared to working with plumbing and electric that was several centuries old," he joked.

"I bet." She glanced around. "I wondered why your

rooms and the bathroom were much newer looking than the entryway and the other parts of the house that I've seen in pictures."

"The rest of the château is preserved for events and historical purposes. But here, in the family wing, we did what we wanted to make it more comfortable."

"I like it." She ran her hands over his chest. "I like this too." She enjoyed the way his muscles seemed to jump under her light touch.

"You're driving me crazy," he said before he kissed her.

"Good." She sighed and wrapped herself around him.

The drive back into Paris seemed to take longer than the drive out to the château. Maybe because this time she wasn't entertained by Blake's kisses? Instead, she watched the dark countryside. Less than ten minutes after they started driving, the sun rose over the city.

"Wow. I've been to Paris more times than I can count, but I've never seen the sunrise over the city before," she admitted.

"It's a lot different than a sunset," he said. "For one, there are a hell of a lot fewer people out and about."

"Somehow it makes it a lot nicer," she admitted as they drove through the empty streets.

"In an hour or so there will be thousands of tourists and locals rushing around. But for now, it's all ours." He reached over and took her hand.

She sighed and wondered if he knew just how romantic he was.

When they pulled into her hotel, she was thankful that he parked along the empty street and pulled her into his arms to kiss her.

"I'd like to see you again," he said, and she felt her heart skip with joy.

"I'd like that too." She thought about her schedule. "I'm shooting from eight to noon the next five days. Then I have two days off. It switches to noon to eight the following six days."

"Where are you filming?" he asked.

"All over, really. Two days we're in the Champ de Mars, then we're at the Louvre. They're trying to secure the Château Versailles for the last week of shooting, but I hear it's not going well. We may have to finish the last week in a studio back in the States."

Blake frowned slightly. "What if..." he started but then stopped.

"What?" she asked, not wanting their time to be cut short or, for that matter, for them to be talking about her work.

"What if you could get your hands on another château?"

She blinked and, maybe it was the lack of sleep, but at first she didn't understand him. Then she gasped. "For real?"

He chuckled. "It would be a perfect excuse to see you again."

She kissed him and then sighed. "I'd hoped to see you again tonight."

He frowned slightly. "I have a meeting that will probably run late. If I can swing it." He glanced up at the massive hotel building.

"I'm in the deluxe suite. I'll add you to the approved list of guests." She smiled. "And..." She pulled out her cell phone and sent him her contact info. "Not that I'm desperate or anything," she added with a smile.

He chuckled and pulled her back for another kiss. "The thought hadn't crossed my mind."

Two hours later, she was sitting in makeup being berated by Carlos about the bags under her eyes when Blake's first text came through.

"We forgot your dress this morning. I'm having it delivered to your hotel suite now. Along with a little something else. Don't read too much into it, or, well, if you like it, do. Thanks for bumping into me last night."

She couldn't stop smiling and could practically feel herself vibrating as she remembered what Blake had done to her last night. How he had made her feel. Cherished. More so than anyone else had made her feel.

"Well, well," Carlos said, setting down the makeup brush he held. "Carmen, look at this," he said to his wife.

"Hm?" Carmen glanced up from her task of braiding Robin's long hair.

"Our girl is in love," Carlos said with a smile.

"What?" She blushed slightly. "No, I'm..."

"Oh, look," Carmen said with a soft cheer. "Her eyes are glowing."

Robin rolled her eyes. "There's no such thing."

"My Carmen's eyes glow each time after a night of passion with me," Carlos said with a slight nudge to Robin's shoulder.

"Carlos." Carmen playfully tapped her husband's shoulder with the hairbrush. "Enough teasing." She leaned closer. "Who is the lucky man?"

Carlos and Carmen had been with her from the start of her career. She trusted them more than she did anyone else in the industry and thought of them as family. Still, until she knew that it was okay to tell others about their... relationship, she figured it was best to keep Blake's name out of things.

"I can't be in love. I've only spent one night with him," she said as the duo got back to work.

"It only took one night with me before *mi amor* was hooked," Carlos said with a wink towards Carmen.

"That's because I felt sorry for you," Carmen added with a chuckle.

"Did it?" she asked Carmen. "Did you know after only one night?"

Carmen's playful smile slipped slightly. "No, muchacha, take your time. Carlos came along at a time in my life when..." Her eyes moved up to her husband's. "I needed him the most. I was very lucky to find him. We are *almas gemelas*. Soulmates," she finished with a smile. "But you will know yours when you meet him, no matter how long it takes you."

"Right." She sank back into the chair and thought about those words the rest of the day.

CHAPTER FOUR

"I don't care how long it takes," Blake said over the phone. "If they say it's needed, then get it in the budget," he said before hanging up.

"Problems?" Leslie Cooper, one of his personal assistants, asked.

A short time ago, when Leslie had been hired on in his office, a rumor had gone around that the two of them were an item.

The woman was ex-military, which looked good in the press, and she was easy enough on the eyes. But she lacked the morals for his taste. In the first week after she'd been hired, he'd witnessed just how low she would stoop to go places in the business. Ever since, he'd decided to keep his distance and had even tasked Jeffery, another one of his long-standing PAs, to keep an eye on her.

"No," he answered Leslie. "Nothing that hasn't been handled at this point." He took the folder she offered him.

"Your next meeting is with the prime minister of..." She glanced down at her binder.

"Sweden," he offered, already knowing his schedule.

"Right." Leslie sighed and then proceeded to drone on about the rest of his schedule, as if he hadn't memorized it already.

Sitting in meeting after meeting and not having even a second to think about Robin was pure torture. How the hell was he supposed to concentrate when she'd sent back a text of her smiling at the bouquet of cream roses that he'd sent her?

He wanted to spend the rest of his trip in Paris with her. Already, he'd extended his trip another week so that he could spend time with her. Even if she didn't convince her producer to film at his family's château, he'd convinced himself that he was going to do whatever it took to spend as much time with her as possible.

As he'd expected, his last meeting finished a few hours after dinnertime. He'd packed a bag so the twenty-minute drive to the château didn't eat up more of his time.

He sent Robin a text and started to head towards her hotel.

"I'm done for the day. Hope your shooting went well. If you're free, I'd like to see you?"

Even if she'd changed her mind, at least he would be able to get a room for the night and get a few hours of sleep before he was set to start with more meetings the next day.

Her text reply came moments later. "Looking forward to seeing you again. Come on over. Have you eaten?"

He answered the text via his car's system.

"Almost there. Missed dinner. I was thinking of grabbing a sandwich on my way up."

Her response was quick. "I'll take care of the food. See you soon."

He pulled into the hotel's valet parking and was too

busy getting his car checked in and his bag from the trunk to see the photographer.

But by the time he stepped into Robin's suite, he'd received a text message from Leslie and Ken, the heads of his marketing team.

"So, I guess the rumors are true about you and Robin Stein?" Leslie texted.

"Do I need to run block on this Robin Stein situation?" Ken asked.

He was frowning down at Ken's text when Robin answered her door.

"Problems?" she asked, leaning against the doorjamb.

He glanced up and was about to answer her when he noticed what she was wearing. The white silky material of the dress flowed around her shoulders and arms. The skirt ended high up on her thighs leaving her legs completely bare. He didn't know which was sexier, that her legs were bare or that she wasn't wearing any shoes, which showcased her bright, pink-tipped toenails.

"Hi." He tucked his phone into his pocket, forgetting to reply to anyone.

"Hi." She smiled up at him. "Hungry?"

Thoughts of enjoying her, lapping her up, flashed in his mind as he stepped into her room.

"Starved," he admitted as he set his bag down inside the door. He kicked it shut and pulled her into his arms. Covering her lips, he felt her melt against him.

When his stomach growled, he pulled away as she laughed.

"You are hungry." She smiled up at him.

"My meetings ran through lunch and dinner. They only offered snacks. You know, bread, wine." He shrugged. "Nothing much."

"I've ordered room service; it should be here soon." She motioned him into the room.

He looked around and whistled. "Nice digs."

Truth be told, he'd never experienced the deluxe suite of any hotel before. Sure, sometimes he was put up in some nice hotels, but he'd never experienced the kind of suite he was standing in.

"I know." She did a little squeal. "When my agent, Amanda, told me they'd booked me the room, I went online and started drooling at the pictures."

Even growing up spending a few months out of the year in an old castle hadn't prepared him for the amount of gold inlay that filled the suite.

He was used to classic historical furniture, so that didn't surprise him as much as the amount of soft pink and gold everywhere. Even though in his mind it was on the feminine side, the place was gorgeous.

"I guess you go for this sort of thing?" he asked, running his finger over the pink high-back chairs.

She laughed and moved over to stand next to the sofa.

"I wouldn't fill my own home with it, but it is pretty once in a while." She tilted her head. "I suppose it's just like your place. Old things have their place, but when it comes to comfort, how you decorated your rooms are more my speed."

Just hearing those words had him relaxing for some reason. It mattered to him, he realized, what her tastes were. He'd dated a few women with different tastes than him. When the relationships had ended, he'd realized those should have been warning signs.

He went through what he knew about Robin and realized that everything had come from articles. He wasn't even sure any of it was true.

He wanted to spend the next few hours getting to know everything he could about her.

When their food was delivered, he was happily surprised to see that she'd ordered an array of food—chicken, fish, and even beef stew, along with several different side dishes and a tray of desserts.

"I didn't know what you'd like, so I went a little overboard," Robin said after she closed the door to the suite.

He smiled. "I like all of it." He lifted a few more of the lids. "We're going to have plenty."

"I skipped out on lunch too," she said as she sat across from him at the table. "Filming ran long today, and we didn't get done until after five."

"What do you say," he started as they began filling their plates with food, "we get to know one another. You know, outside of what the gossip rags say about us."

She smiled. "I'd like that. You start." She motioned with her fork.

"What's your favorite color?" he asked her, thinking of the first thing that popped into his mind.

She chuckled. "Pink. You?"

"Royal blue."

"That's specific." She leaned on the table slightly.

"My mother messed that up for years. She'd buy me soft blue gifts and even painted my walls robin's egg blue once." He leaned forward and took a roll and then handed her one. She took a bite and then set it on her plate. "Within a year, I finally confessed my preference."

"Noted." She smiled. "Favorite band?"

"Rush," he answered easily.

"Old school," she stated.

"Not according to my father," he joked. "They're timeless."

"Agreed." She nodded. "Floyd is mine."

His smile doubled. "Second favorite here. Movie?"

She laughed. "*Star Wars*. The older ones."

"Duh." He rolled his eyes like his sister did, which had her laughing. "I thought you'd say something more..." He stopped and waved towards the room.

"Oh, don't get me wrong. I like the *Notebook* too, but come on. Lightsabers beat out all romantic plots."

He poured her a glass of the wine that had been delivered. "Red wine." He held up his glass. "Your preference?"

"I like both along with beer. It depends on the mood and the food." She tapped his glass before taking a sip.

"Same." He took a sip as he thought of his next question. "City or small town?"

She frowned and looked as if she was thinking. "Both. City life is easier, but there's just something wonderful about a small town. I grew up in one in Colorado. In Castle Rock, everyone knew everyone else's business." She sighed. "Which was both a good thing and a bad thing." He nodded in agreement. "But living in the city for the past few years, I've grown accustomed to all the perks."

"Such as?" he asked.

"Convenience. If you can't find what you're looking for, you're not looking hard enough." She took a bite of her chicken.

"True. I live in a relatively small town on the outskirts of Atlanta. When I need something specific, I head into the city. I like to help the small local businesses as much as I can, but sometimes you just can't beat the big stores that carry more products."

"Exactly." She motioned with her fork. "We both have sisters. Yours is older, if I remember correctly?"

"Ten years. She's my half-sister. Same dad," he added. "Your sister is younger?"

"Two years," Robin answered. "When our parents divorced, I moved to California with my mother, she stayed behind with our dad." She shrugged. "I see Claire about twice a year." She sighed. "Not enough."

"My sister and her family live about half a mile from my place. If I didn't travel so much, I'd see them more often."

"You mentioned nieces and nephews?" she asked.

"Two nieces and a nephew. Ten, eight, and five," he added with a smile.

She smiled as well. "I bet that's nice being so close to your family."

The tone of her voice had him setting his fork down. "Your parents divorced when you were…"

"Fifteen almost sixteen. Mom was heading to California. I wasn't really given a chance in going with her, but the moment I stepped foot in California, I had a new dream of breaking into acting." She set her fork down and took a sip of her wine. "I got the part for *Raising Molly* a few weeks after moving to California."

"That must have been a good distraction from the family issues." He watched her reaction.

She nodded slowly. "I didn't deal with it until there was a break in filming." She leaned back in her chair. "By that time, my mother had already moved on. She married Kyle, the man she'd moved to Cali for. He works in a gym as a personal trainer."

"What does your sister do? Besides design clothing?" he asked, curious. He vaguely remembered seeing a grainy photo of the two blondes. Robin was taller but the sisters were closer in appearance than most sisters.

Robin's smile grew. "Claire is going to design school.

Already, she's more talented than a lot of the big names in Hollywood."

He couldn't help but smile as she started talking about her sister. He could feel the love oozing from her the more she talked about Claire.

CHAPTER FIVE

R obin felt more relaxed the longer she talked with Blake. For the next hour, as they slowly ate, they talked about family and their past. She learned a lot about Blake and his family in that hour and easily told him about her own life.

Since she'd become famous, she'd never really opened up to anyone as much as she did him. For the first time in years, she felt at ease about it.

Maybe it was because she knew Blake had also had to deal with people digging into his past, searching for dirt or something shocking to expose. In her case, for the first few years of her career, they'd chosen to highlight her parents' divorce.

For Blake, she knew it always circled back to his kidnapping case. Several articles tried to peg him as a mentally damaged child-man, incapable of doing the job he'd been elected to do. All of which he'd quickly squashed by his actions and how well he'd maintained himself under fire.

They moved over to the sofa, and he tossed off his shoes, tie, and jacket. He even rolled up the sleeves of his shirt, showcasing his tan arms. The relaxed look on him was far sexier than the all-business look he'd had when he'd arrived.

She was having a difficult time keeping her eyes from him, or from wanting him. It took all her willpower to stop herself from reaching out and touching him.

They laughed over old stories of their school years and their families, and when he pulled her legs up onto his lap, she snuggled down and enjoyed him running his hands slowly over her.

She couldn't remember the last time she'd felt so compelled to enjoy a man before. Had she ever? Vaguely, she wondered if Blake was putting off some highly concentrated pheromones. She laughed at herself when she owned up to the fact that it had been over eight months since she'd dated anyone seriously.

"What's so funny?" he asked softly.

"Hm, you, me, this." She motioned with her wine glass. She noticed it was empty and set it down.

"Oh? What's funny about us being here, like this?" He hands stilled on her thigh.

"Hm." She closed her eyes and rolled her head back. God, his hands felt so good on her skin. Okay, maybe one too many glasses of wine. "I was just wondering what kind of spell you have over me to make me want you so much."

His hand started moving upward slowly. "It's you who has a spell on me. I should be getting a few hours of rest before I have to start with meetings again in the morning. But I'm here, with you, wishing to spend as much time learning about you as I can."

"Blake?" she said, laying her hand over his and nudging it higher.

"Yes," his voice was only a whisper.

"I think we've done enough talking for tonight." She

pulled him down towards her. When his mouth covered hers, she groaned and melted against him.

When his fingers found her wetness, she arched into him as he dipped them into her, causing her entire body to go on edge. How could she want him so badly?

She reached for him and unzipped his dress pants. She found him gloriously hard. She had to have him, or she'd burst into a million pieces.

Sliding up, she straddled his hips as his hands gripped her waist. When she slid down onto his full length, his name was a moan of pure pleasure.

"Never," she said into his shoulder. "It's never been like this." She started to move over him.

"No, never," he agreed as his fingers dug into her hips, pulling her closer. When his mouth took hers, she knew that it could never be like this with anyone else. How in the hell had she fallen for Blake so quickly?

When her alarm went off the next morning, she rolled over to find Blake already sitting up on the edge of the bed.

"Sorry, that's mine," he said, shutting off his phone alarm.

Checking the clock, she groaned. "Mine's about to go off in five minutes."

He leaned over and placed a soft kiss on her lips. "Today shouldn't be as long as yesterday."

She smiled. "Ditto."

"Dinner?" he asked.

"Yes, but a real one. Out somewhere." She thought about it. "Le Cinq or how about Pur'?"

"Either or. I can have my PA make reservations." He walked towards the bathroom with her on his heels.

"Le Cinq, let's say..." She quickly calculated the time and the day ahead of her. "Six o'clock?"

He smiled and stepped into the shower beside her. "Six it is." Then he was kissing her, and she once more forgot time and place as she lost herself in his embrace.

Almost an hour later, she glided into the trailer and gasped at the number of white roses that greeted her.

"What's all this?" Carlos and Carmen asked moments later when they stepped inside to start their daily ritual.

"Can you believe this?" she asked cheerfully as she buried her face in the white petals.

"From your mystery man?" Carlos asked.

"Not such a mystery any longer," Carmen said, nudging her husband in the ribs.

"Right." Carlos' smile grew as his eyebrows wiggled. "So the rumors are true? You and that senator?"

"Rumors?" Robin asked as her smile slipped.

"Chica, didn't you see?" Carmen rushed towards her and pulled out her phone. When she turned the screen around, there was an image of Robin and Blake kissing and embracing with the lit Eiffel Tower behind them. Carmen sighed. "You're already being dubbed the most romantic couple of the year. Rumors are going around that you've secretly been dating for months. But we know better."

She shook her head and let out a heavy sigh. "I've only been with him two nights. Rumors are rumors."

"Two nights can seem like an eternity when it's meant," Carmen said with a smile towards her husband.

"Enough gossip," Carlos said after kissing his wife. "We are running out of time. They will be expecting you soon."

Half an hour later, she stepped onto the set and allowed her character, Meg, to take over her personality and thoughts. Meg was a twenty-something woman in Paris for the first time. She was in awe of all that surrounded her, including the man of her dreams, Roger, played by Tom

Levi, an actor who had starred in more than six romantic comedies in the past five years.

Tom was perfect for the role of Roger, the suave millionaire recluse who didn't trust anyone. But Meg's honesty and obvious annoyance towards Roger's wealth breaks his outer tough shell, allowing the couple to fall madly in love.

So far, they had filmed all of the scenes except for one of the last at the Eiffel Tower and the scene where they meet for the first time at a formal event, which they'd hoped to film at the Château Versailles.

During their first break for the day, the director, Marcus Burgess, who was a staple in Hollywood, called a quick meeting. Since filming had started almost six months ago, she'd grown to like Marcus more than any other director she'd worked with. The man knew his stuff.

She remembered a few years back hearing about his difficulties with his first marriage. There had been a big scandal when his first wife had accused him of having an affair with Amber Scott. But then Marcus had come forward and stepped out of the closet. Now, he was married to his longtime love, Ramon. The happy duo was one of Hollywood's top gay power couples. Ramon owned and ran one of the best restaurants in LA while Marcus continued to put out more hit movies than any other director in his field.

"It appears as if the Château Versailles is a no-go. We're trying to secure a ballroom... somewhere." The man rolled his eyes and sighed.

"I might have a place..." she said before thinking it through. Then everyone's eyes turned to her. "Château de Ferrières," she added before she could back down. Even though her face heated, she continued. "Mr. Rhodes has graciously invited the company to film and offered to give us the run of the place. He even suggested we could secure rooms for the week so we wouldn't have to commute during filming."

There were several excited exclamations before Marcus held up his hands to quiet everyone again.

Marcus smiled. "So, it appears as if some of the rumors are true then."

She couldn't help the smile. "Not all, but enough that it allows us a beautiful château to film in."

"If you can give Steph Mr. Rhodes' contact info, she can set everything up," Marcus said, motioning to his assistant.

Robin nodded as Steph walked over to her. She gave the woman Blake's PA's number, which he'd given her earlier that morning before they'd parted ways.

When the filming continued for the day, she found it difficult to focus on being Meg. So much so that filming dragged on until a quarter past three.

Frustrated that she now had less time than she'd hoped to go shopping for a new dress before her dinner date, she unlocked her trailer and was so preoccupied with wondering what to wear for the night that at first the destruction inside didn't faze her.

Every surface in her trailer was splattered red, and the white rose petals were destroyed. She gasped and almost fell backward off the steps.

"Miss Stein, Marcus wanted me to..." Steph said, walking towards her. When the young woman saw Robin's face, she rushed forward and gripped her arm. "What's wrong?"

"My.... trailer," Robin managed to get out.

Steph glanced in and then gasped before pulling out a walkie-talkie. "We need security over at Miss Stein's trailer ASAP." She gripped Robin's arm and started walking her towards the staging area, where Marcus was still talking to some of the crew.

Robin glanced back at her trailer as two security guards rushed inside.

"Someone destroyed her trailer," Steph said, breaking into Marcus's conversation. Steph nudged her into a chair. "I'll get you some water," she said and quickly disappeared.

"Oh, sweetie." Marcus rushed over to take her hand. "Are you okay?"

"My... roses. They splattered red paint all over. Everything." She closed her eyes and felt her head spin.

For the next fifteen minutes, she sat in a complete haze as everyone crowded around her to comfort her. Marcus decided to drive her back to her hotel himself. When she mentioned she had a dinner date and didn't even have a dress, he parked outside of Giorgio Armani, then walked into the store with her.

"I'm not letting you out of my sight until your man picks you up for your date," he promised her.

She held onto his arm for support as she walked through the store in a daze.

"This one," Marcus told the clerk, holding up a black dress. "You can never have too many LBDs," he said with a smile.

The clerk looked at her and asked. "Size..." The woman ran her eyes over her. "Six?"

Robin nodded. "Yes, thank you." She could tell the woman was judging her, even though they were roughly the same size. How many times over the years had she been accused of being too heavy, too thin, too short, or even too tall? It appeared that no matter what she was, someone was going to have an opinion about it. Which is why she never let it bother her.

Just last year, she'd publicly spoken out against a magazine that had seriously altered her image. She couldn't allow the industry to shame the young audience members into feeling self-conscious about themselves because of unrealistic industry standards.

When she slipped the dress on, she knew that it would more than do for the night. The soft material hugged her like a second skin.

For the first time in almost an hour, she thought of something other than the destruction she'd witnessed. Just thinking of spending her evening with Blake again had her smiling. When she walked out of the changing room, dress in hand, Marcus smiled at her.

"There she is." He wrapped an arm around her. "I knew that shopping would bring you back from the darkness."

"Thanks." She hugged him. "You're the best."

Marcus chuckled. "Anything to keep your man happy. We're all set to start filming at his place in two days, and I want to make sure you keep him happy."

CHAPTER SIX

When Robin stepped into the lobby wearing the tight black dress and spiky heels, he almost swallowed his tongue. Her legs appeared longer, sexier than he remembered they had felt wrapped around him.

Her long hair was tied in a braid that hung over her bare shoulder. Her lips were painted a sexy deep red.

"Evening," she purred as she stopped in front of him.

"Hi." He felt his throat close up. "You look..." He blinked and was surprised to realize that he didn't know exactly what to say. 'Amazing' didn't cut it. "Wow," he finished.

Her smile almost tipped the scales to him rushing her back upstairs and skipping dinner. Then she took his arm and started walking towards the doors.

"I can't tell you how much I need tonight," she sighed as they stepped outside.

"Oh?" He figured he'd keep his statements to one or two words, at least until his brain started functioning again.

"Yes. I loved the roses you sent me," she said, but he could hear the strain in her tone.

He opened the rented car's door for her, then slid behind the wheel. "But?"

"I'm afraid someone broke into my trailer and destroyed them."

He was thankful he hadn't started driving away yet. He turned towards her. "Are you okay?"

"I wasn't there." She touched his hand. "The only casualty was pretty much everything in my trailer and the flowers."

"I'm sorry." He frowned. "Does that happen to you often?" He ran his eyes over her face and searched for any signs of distress but could only see how beautiful she was.

"No, never." She shrugged slightly. "A few stalker-y type notes, but nothing this... desperate before."

"You have security on the set, right?" he asked as he pulled out into traffic while he thought about checking into the situation himself. He knew a guy personally that was perfect for the job. GI Joe.

"Yes." She waved her hand towards him. "Marcus has assured me that it was probably just a one-off type of deal. They probably didn't even know it was my trailer since none of them are marked, for privacy reasons. One of Marcus's requirements after an incident that happened way back when he'd been working with Amber Scott."

"Wow, your director has worked with Amber Scott?" He thought of the Hollywood A-lister blonde bombshell. The woman was everywhere now. Even after having two kids, she was in a ton of good movies and even a few television shows. He liked them all.

"Yes, a few times." Robin smiled. "Jealous?"

"Amber Scott is... well, Amber Scott." He wiggled his eyebrows at her as he pulled up to the valet at Le Cinq.

"I know it. Even I have her on my freebie list," she said before getting out of the car.

He was chuckling and holding Robin's hand when the first flash went off. Trying to shield her from the onslaught of flashes that followed, he rushed them towards the doors and the safety inside the restaurant.

"How did they know we were coming?" he mumbled when they were safely inside.

"They always seem to know." Robin sighed and held onto his arm. "I'm so sorry."

He stopped and turned to her. "This is in no way your fault." He waited until she nodded before turning and checking in with the maître d'.

They were seated on one of the small square tables with crisp white tablecloths and high-back chairs, far away from the windows. The room was massive and filled with people who appeared to have zero interest in them, and he relaxed his guard.

"Does that always happen to you?" he asked after the waiter poured them each a glass of water and gave them a moment to decide on their drinks.

"Yes," she said, and he noticed her slump a little in her chair. "But not as bad here as in the States." She shook her head and leaned forward. "What kind of wine shall we get?"

"Change of subject." He nodded. "Okay." He glanced at the menu. "I suppose it depends on if you're having the fish special or the beef." He glanced up at her over the menu.

"Fish," she said quickly. "You?"

"Same." He smiled. "Then..." He ran his eyes over the wine list and rattled off three options for her to choose from.

"A man who knows wine." She set her menu down and

ran her eyes over him. "What other hidden talents do you possess?"

He smiled and thought for a moment. "I'm pretty good at baking."

Her eyebrows shot up as she leaned forward. "I'd love to hear how that came about."

During the hour and a half meal, they dove deeper into each other's pasts. He opened up to her about things he didn't even think were important. Yet she hung on every word, as did he when she talked about her life with her sister.

She mentioned her sister Claire more than she mentioned her parents, something he was dying to ask about, but the night was going too well to put a damper on her mood.

"I hear we're all moving out to your place in two days." She smiled over her wine glass. Their empty plates had been cleared long ago.

"My PAs have assured me there will be enough room for everyone. Including all the equipment. They've been working with the château's staff." He smiled. "Did you know that most of the staff at the place are multigenerational? Some have family members that worked at the château almost one-hundred and fifty years ago."

She shook her head as her eyes grew big. "I can't imagine. I don't even know what my grandparents did for a living."

He chuckled. "Me either."

She glanced around and then sighed. "I suppose they want us out of here soon."

He glanced at his watch and winced. "You have an early morning." She nodded. "Yeah, so do I. Unfortunately. I'll take you back to your hotel."

She smiled. "Just because we can't spend the night in the same bed, doesn't mean things are over."

"Hm?" he asked.

She chuckled. "The look on your face." She shook her head. "Heartbreak." She placed her hands over her chest.

He smiled and moved to pull out her chair for her as she stood up.

"I was hoping to find out what you were wearing under this." He ran a finger over the strap of her dress.

She turned and wrapped her arms around his shoulders. "I was hoping to show you." She kissed him lightly since they were standing in the middle of the restaurant. Even though the place had emptied in the past half hour, there were still people around.

He took her hand in his, and they walked towards the doors. "What are the chances we waited long enough for the cameras to go away?"

"Unfortunately, not high enough for a bet," she answered.

He sighed. "I thought not."

Once again, the moment they stepped outside, they were bombarded with flashes and questions. Thankfully, the rental car had been retrieved before they'd stepped out.

He opened her door for her and was rushing around to get inside the driver's side when the back window of the rental exploded. People screamed and ran, pushing him away from the passenger door, away from Robin. He fought for what seemed like minutes before he was able to free himself from the rushing crowd to return to the car and yank open her door.

He instantly worried when he saw her bent over on the seat, but then she glanced up at him. Her face was pale, and shards of glass covered her entire body.

"Are you okay?" he asked, kneeling beside her.

"Yes. You?" she asked, looking around as everyone continued to scatter.

"Yes, let's..." He moved to cover her this time when the window on the open door beside them shattered, sending more glass raining over them.

"Someone's shooting at us," she cried out. She pulled him into the car and tried to shield their bodies as best as she could. He didn't know if he was shielding her or if she was trying to protect him from any further shots.

The silence was almost deafening, and the seconds seemed to stretch on forever. They cowered there until the sirens became so loud that his head ached. He thought Robin would cry, but she just held onto him, as if she was trying to keep him from leaving her and getting in harm's way.

"Sir," someone said in French to them. "It's safe to come out now." He glanced over at the male officer and noticed there were four other men in black uniforms standing beside the car, scanning the area. "We've searched the area."

He climbed out of the car and reached to help Robin out. Her eyes were huge. Her beautifully braided hair was now messy, and her dark eye makeup ran down her cheeks, assuring him she'd cried silently as they'd waited.

"Are you okay?" he asked, pulling her into his arms.

"Yes," she whispered, holding onto him.

"You're bleeding," one of the officers said. "Let's get a medic over here."

Blake tensed, and his arms around Robin tightened. Had she been hit? Was she bleeding? He pulled back and ran his eyes over every inch of her. Then he noticed her eyes zoned in on his arm. Her hands moved up and gripped the sleeve of his dress shirt.

At first, he didn't register anything, then he felt a dull stinging on his skin under his dress shirt.

"It's just a cut," he assured her. "From the glass." He ripped the sleeve of his shirt and exposed the scratched skin. "It's not even deep." He showed her.

"Americans?" the cop asked them.

"Yes," Robin answered for them as she started pulling him towards the flashing lights of the ambulance.

He sat in the back of the ambulance, listening to Robin tell the police what had happened as the medic bandaged up his forearm. When she was done, the medic told him that he wouldn't need stitches, but to keep an eye on the wound.

"Well, this was a fun way to end the night," he said as they climbed into a cab.

"I can't even wrap my head around what happened." She leaned her head against his shoulder.

The fact was, he could wrap his mind around what had just happened. There was no doubt, in his opinion, what someone had been shooting at. So, while Robin had been talking to the police, he'd sent a 911 text to his brother-in-law.

Ethan had replied quickly and assured him that he would be on the next plane to Paris and would meet them at the château. He even mentioned that he'd be bringing his longtime business partner, Javan.

For as long as Blake could remember, the huge Jamaican man had been one of his favorite people on the planet. In the past few years, he'd seen less and less of the man. He'd married Jenna a few years back and they'd had a daughter, Chloe, who was almost five now.

He'd missed the man and thankfully knew that his brother-in-law bringing Javan meant they weren't going to mess around.

"What now?" Robin asked when the cab pulled in front of her hotel, and they noticed even more paparazzi out front.

He pulled her tighter against his body. "Now you pack up and move in with me until my bodyguards get here."

CHAPTER SEVEN

Robin was too tired and too concerned that someone had just tried to assassinate Blake to argue. The truth was, she'd been dying to get back to the château. She'd hoped he'd ask her again, but not like this. He must have believed that she was in danger because of him.

"Is this everything?" he asked her almost an hour later when her four large suitcases were packed.

"Yes." She glanced around and set her large makeup container on top of one of the suitcases.

"You travel light," he said, wheeling two of the cases towards the door.

She chuckled and thought of all the extra outfits she'd packed that she hadn't even worn yet. "This is light?"

"You should see how my mother and sister pack. It's why we all determined long ago to keep a second wardrobe at the château." He muscled the two cases out the door.

She pushed the other two through the doorway just as a bellboy arrived to help.

"Your new rental car is downstairs," the bellboy said to Blake.

"Thank you." He took over her two cases. She grabbed her makeup kit and followed them into the elevator.

She'd changed out of her new sexy black dress into a pair of comfortable jeans, a sweatshirt, and some of her favorite tennis shoes. Blake had grabbed one of her ball caps and set it on her head.

"It might help." He shrugged.

She tucked her hair through the hole and added a pair of sunglasses, which, when she thought about it was completely stupid, since it was past midnight and would be pitch dark outside.

When they stepped outside, she noticed a few things. The first was that security had cleared the street out front. The second was that his new rental was a black SUV instead of a sports car.

After her luggage was in the back, she sat back and relaxed as he started driving out of the city. Her phone rang less than ten minutes later.

"It's Marcus," she said to Blake before answering.

"Why didn't you call me?" Marcus said when she answered. "Are you okay?"

"Yes, I'm fine." She relaxed back and closed her eyes. "Everything happened so fast. We're on our way to the château. Blake thinks it's best if I stay there with him."

"I agree," Marcus broke in quickly. "I'll see about rearranging the schedule. I think we have enough done that we won't need you again until we get up to the château."

She opened her eyes. "But I thought we had to reshoot—"

"I'll make it work," Marcus broke in again. "Your safety is the number one priority."

"My..." She frowned. "It's Blake they were after." She glanced at Blake through the darkness.

"Oh, honey," Marcus said with a sigh.

When the silence stretched on, she thought about it. Really thought. "You think..." She felt the blood drain. Blake reached over and took her free hand and he gave it a light squeeze. "They weren't after you?" she asked Blake.

"I'll let you two discuss this. Be safe. I'll see you in two days," Marcus said quickly and then hung up.

She tucked her phone into her purse. "Why didn't I think about it. The break-in at my trailer." She closed her eyes and felt tears roll down her cheeks again. "Because of me, you almost got shot."

"Not because of you," Blake said firmly. "You had nothing to do with it."

"No," she said softly with a sigh.

His hand disappeared as he turned a corner and entered the highway, then it was back holding hers as they continued towards the château.

"Marcus has given me the next two days off," she said as she watched the lights of the city fade.

"That's good. I'm going to cancel the rest of my meetings," he said, surprising her.

"Can you do that? I mean, people have come from all over the world for this conference." She instantly started feeling guilty.

"I've said my peace already. If they need me, they know where to find me. Besides, when what happened tonight gets out, I'm sure no one will complain if I'm absent for a few more meetings."

"True," she agreed. They grew quiet and at one point she must have fallen asleep. She woke up when the car slowed.

"Sorry," he said softly. "I know you're probably exhausted."

"I didn't mean to fall asleep." She glanced out the front window.

Just seeing the château, with all the lights making the sandstone walls to glow, had her stomach bubbling with anticipation. This time, even though she was still tired, she wanted to explore every inch of the place. Well, every inch that she could in a single night.

"I'd like that tour," she said, leaning forward.

"Sure," he agreed as he parked at the front door.

Last time, she hadn't noticed anyone around the massive place. This time, however, two men in dark suits stood at the entrance, waiting for them. When the car turned off, they rushed forward and gathered her luggage from the back.

"That is Jean and Thomas." Blake motioned to the men. "I'll wait and introduce you to the rest of the staff in the morning. For now, I'll give you the grand tour." He held out his arm and she tucked hers into his, making sure to be careful around the bandages.

"Does it hurt?" she asked him as they stepped through the outer arches and inside. The marble half-circle staircases loomed just inside the doors.

He glanced down at his arm and shrugged. "To be honest, I'd forgotten all about it. As I said, it was just a scratch." They stopped just inside the doors. "The main staircases." He motioned with his free hand.

"I saw this part before," she said with a chuckle.

"Right." He nodded and moved to the right staircase. They climbed and then turned right down a hallway instead of heading into the main room as they had before. He stopped and opened a set of double doors. "The parlor."

She wanted to drink everything in, but to be honest, there was just so much. Her eyes bounced between the blue walls, the gold and white ceilings, the decorative rugs, and the art. So much art.

"How did your family come into this place?" she asked as they moved into what Blake called the salon. This room had similar decorations as before, only these walls were a soft cream color, as was the furniture, giving the room a far more feminine atmosphere.

"An exchange of sorts." He shrugged. "My father is gray on the details." He leaned closer to her. "I've always thought it was a deal gone wrong. But my mother and my father's lawyers tell me the exchange was on the up and up." He winked at her. "There are a total of ten staircases, along with more than eighty suites in the château. The basement level, the floor we walked in on, is reserved for staff and storage. More than a dozen full-time staff are on hand at any time. For events we could have hundreds. Only half a dozen of the long-term ones live here full time." He continued as they walked down another hallway, past a smaller set of stairs. "This is technically the second floor, but it's called the premier étage." They turned down another hallway. "We are walking around the main hall." He motioned towards a set of tall wooden doors. "On this level, you can exit the back of the property by the outdoor grand staircase."

"I've seen that staircase in pictures." She remembered the wide stone steps with large lion statues on either side. The gardens on-site were beautiful. Rumored to be one of the best in France.

"We'll save that tour for daylight," he said, turning another corner. "The main study, which leads to the library." She followed him through a dark wood-paneled room and then watched as he pushed a panel and the wall slid open silently. They stepped through and walked out onto a catwalk overlooking a two-story library.

She held in a gasp. She'd never seen pictures of the library before. This room was so beautiful, she held her breath as she looked around.

There was an intricate wood circular staircase with a red carpet that wound down to the main floor. The upper floor held floor-to-ceiling bookshelves packed with books. Two large windows were covered by dark green and gold curtains, but she figured they would let in enough light during the day to read by. High-back chairs sat around a small table and each window had a cushioned window seat she could just imagine enjoying.

She walked over to the dark cherry railing and looked down into the main room.

The wall-to-wall bookshelves were packed with old titles and filled each wall except the one that held a huge stone fireplace. Long cozy-looking brown leather sofas sat facing each other in the middle of the room with a large wood coffee table in the middle. Books were stacked everywhere there was a free space.

A massive gold chandelier hung over the center of the room. Art and statues filled any empty spaces where there weren't books. She wanted to spend more time here. A lot more time.

She glanced over her shoulder and joked. "I thought it would be bigger."

He chuckled. "The previous owner wasn't too big on reading," he joked back.

"No?" She chuckled and shook her head, then she turned towards him. "What about you?" she asked as she leaned on the railing.

He smiled. "I live for a cold night when I can sit down and enjoy a good book in front of a fire."

She sighed and glanced around the room. "That sounds... amazing."

"It's a date for tomorrow night then." He took her hand. "I spent most of my time here as a kid in this room. We'll cut the rest of this floor's tour short. The morning room and dining rooms are better in the daylight." He led her down the circular staircase. "We're in the west wing now, normally filled with guests either hosting weddings or big charity events. For now, it's all empty and ready for your crew to arrive in two days."

"I hope you didn't have to cancel anyone's special day?" she asked, finally feeling tired.

"No, the schedule was blocked out for my trip over a year ago," he explained as they reached the top floor. They circled the main hall once more and passed so many doors, she lost track. Once they passed another large marble staircase, she thought she remembered that his room was the second door down another hallway. When he turned and then opened the door, she silently cheered her memory.

Stepping into his room, she once again looked around. Her luggage sat inside, along the wall next to where his walk-in closet was.

He had a sitting room that he'd decorated in simple earth colors. A leather sofa faced a flat-screen television over a modern-looking gas fireplace. There was a huge cherry desk behind the sofa, facing away from the windows. The sleeping portion of his bedroom was much smaller than this room, and it wasn't until she mentally made note of the massive place that she realized that it was because it was one of the four towers.

"You sleep in a castle tower," she said with a half

chuckle. "Like a prince." She wrapped her arms around him.

He chuckled. "I just spent most of my summers in my youth here. Mainly, the château is an investment property for my family, something my mother can brag about at social events."

"Right." She smiled as she stifled a yawn.

"Why don't we get settled?" He kissed her. "I can see you are beat."

She nodded and followed him towards her suitcases. They spent the next few moments rolling her luggage into his massive walk-in closet, where she pulled out a few items and hung them. Blake had disappeared and she could hear him on the phone in the next room, so she pulled on her soft purple silk pajama shorts and tank top.

When she stepped out, Blake hung up the phone. He'd removed his jacket, shoes, and tie. He looked as tired as she felt.

Walking over, she wrapped her arms around him and held on.

"Come on," he said into her hair, "let's crawl into bed."

He pulled back the covers of the massive bed and she climbed in. He tossed off his pants and his shirt and crawled in after her. When he pulled her into his arms, she settled against his chest.

"I don't think I've ever been that scared in my life," she admitted.

He was silent for a moment. "You handled yourself pretty well."

She remembered what he'd gone through as a child and closed her eyes tighter. "The truth is, we both need to realize that this could have been about you tonight."

He sighed. "Yeah, but chances are..."

She shifted and looked down at him in the darkness. "Someone breaking into my trailer and splattering red paint over all of my things is a one-time thing. You've been receiving threats since you took office. I know, I've heard about them in the news. Not to mention the kidnapping when you were eight."

He lifted his hand and ran his fingers through her hair, then cupped her face. "It's why I wanted you here. I know there's a chance this is about me. But I couldn't take the chance it was about you and leave you alone in the city." He pulled her down for a soft kiss. "Not when there is this..." He sighed softly. "Between us."

She rested her forehead on his as she felt her heart jump in her chest.

CHAPTER EIGHT

B lake knew that it would be only a matter of time before the place was full of people. Two days was nowhere near enough time to spend with someone he had very strong feelings towards.

Hell, who was he fooling. He was falling for her, and hard.

He was slightly surprised when Robin woke him up around eight o'clock the following morning by running her hands over his chest and trailing her lips down his neck.

He wrapped his arms around her, rolled over, and snuggled into her hair.

"God, you smell good," he mumbled as his hands started to move over her soft warm body.

She chuckled and then moaned when he kissed her until they were both breathless. When he slid into her, he knew that he was home. She felt right. So right. As if they had been made for one another. How had he lived before she'd come into his life?

He wanted to tell her how he felt, but something kept

him from saying those words he'd only ever uttered to his family before.

When they settled down and were lying naked in each other's arms, he glanced towards the windows.

"It looks like it's a beautiful day out there. What do you say we have some breakfast and then go for a ride?" he asked.

She sat up and looked down at him. "You have horses here?"

He chuckled. "Over half a dozen, actually." He tossed his legs over the bed and stood. "They too are multigenerational. Duke the tenth, the stud horse, is a direct descendant of Duke the fist, one of the first horses brought onto the property." She followed him into the bathroom, and he finished telling her about the barn full of thoroughbreds as they showered.

When they stepped out, he glanced down at the soaked white bandages the medic had placed over his cuts last night.

She took his arm and removed the soaked bandages, then looked at his wounds.

"They don't look too bad. Do you have Band-Aids?" she asked.

"Med kit is under the sink." He motioned to the double sinks.

He leaned against the counter, a towel wrapped around his waist, as she gently replaced the white bandage with a few Band-Aids.

While she worked, he realized that he couldn't imagine feeling this much for anyone else so quickly.

He knew the story of how his sister and brother-in-law had met and fallen in love. Their wild trek through the jungles of Brazil had forged a bond so strong that even now, more than a dozen years later, they were still obsessed with one another.

This was how he was starting to feel about Robin, and he would be stupid if it didn't scare him a little.

They dressed and, while she dried her hair in his bathroom, he opened his laptop and answered a few emails.

When her cell phone ring, he tried not to eavesdrop, but the walls were so thin, he overheard her talking to her agent, Amanda. Robin relayed what had happened the night before and how Marcus had given her the next couple of days off to recoup.

"You don't have to—" Robin started, then grew silent for a while, no doubt while Amanda talked. "Okay, I'll make sure there's plenty of room for you. It will be nice seeing you in a few days."

Without waiting to hear the rest, he picked up the house phone and called down to Arthur, the château's general manager.

"Morning, sir," Arthur said with his thick French accent.

"Morning, Arthur. It appears we'll need one more room prepared," he said, shutting down his computer.

"Yes, sir," Arthur replied.

"We'll be heading down soon for breakfast," he added.

"Everything will be ready," Arthur said before hanging up.

When Robin stepped out of the bathroom in a pair of black pants and a T-shirt, a pair of hiking boots, and her hair in a long braid, he smiled.

"Ready for a day of adventure?" He walked over and kissed her.

She chuckled. "Yes, please." Then she leaned back and ran her eyes over his dark jeans and shirt. He had a pair of riding boots in his closet but had chosen a pair of hiking boots himself since he only planned on a short ride and a long walk around the grounds.

"Wow, I think they picked the wrong outfit for your sexiest man picture." She ran her finger over his biceps.

He laughed then took her hand. "Breakfast is waiting." He kissed her again. "But I'd love to..." He started walking her back to the bedroom as her cell phone rang again.

They groaned at the same time, and he stood back while she answered a call. Instantly, he knew it was her sister when her face lit up.

"Claire," she answered cheerfully. Then she frowned as her sister talked.

"I was going to call you this morning." She glanced at her watch. "What time is it there?" She cringed. "Okay, so I could have called you earlier, but—" She paused. "No, it didn't happen—" There was another pause in the conversation as Robin's eyes ran to his. "Yes, he's fine. It's just cuts." Another pause and Robin smiled. "Yes, that part is true." She held up a finger and then said. "I'm going to put you on speaker since he's only getting my side of this conversation." She punched the button on the phone and her sister's voice filled the room.

"Hi, Blake Rhodes, sexiest man alive last year. This is Robin's little sister, Claire. I just have to say... Thank you!" The last part was almost a scream. "For saving my stupid bigger sister's life."

He smiled. "Actually, your stupid bigger sister saved my life last night," he said, pulling Robin into his arms again. "She pulled me into the car when the second shot shattered the window by my head."

"Oh my god." Claire gasped. "Are you sure you're okay?"

"Like your stupid sister said"—Robin pinched his arm, making him smile— "I just have a few cuts. Which she cleaned and rebandaged for me this morning."

"Are you really staying at Château de Ferrières?" Claire asked.

Robin answered this one. "Yes, and it's amazing. You should see the library. Blake is going to give me the grand tour today, which you are slowing down."

"Oh, don't let me take up any of your tour time. I just had to know that you were okay. Both of you," Claire added.

"We are," Robin answered.

"Later we can talk about what Marcus is going to do about adding extra security," Claire said.

"I've added some extra of my own for your sister," Blake broke in. "They are arriving later this morning and, until things cool off, I won't be leaving your sister's side. Unless she wants me to," he added with a wink to Robin.

He thought he heard Claire sigh before she responded. "Keep me posted. Robin, you have my permission to give the sexiest man alive my cell number."

"Back off, sister," Robin replied with a chuckle.

Claire laughed. "Love you. Keep her safe," she said before hanging up.

"Nice sister," he said as they made their way down to the dining hall.

"Yes. Someday, maybe you can meet her face-to-face," Robin said.

"I'd like that," he responded as they stepped into the main dining hall.

Normally, the large room was packed with hundreds of people, an entire army of staff rushing around taking orders and delivering food and drinks. Today, it was empty except for Jean and Thomas, who stood ready by the only set table.

"Morning," he said to the men as he held a white leather chair for Robin to sit in.

"Wow, this room," Robin said, looking around. "That chandelier." She gasped, looking above them. "It's amazing."

He glanced around the room and had to admit, the dining hall was one of the best rooms in the house. It had been cleaned up long before his father had purchased the place. The massive fairy painting on the ceiling was from one of the top French artists of the nineteenth century. If he thought about it, he could probably come up with the guy's name.

The chandelier was actually from Germany, or so his father had been told. In the center of the room sat a large four-directional sofa, with a water fountain in the middle. Six tall, arched windows filled one wall with white columns on the opposite. The doors had high marble arches above them and each one boasted a unique carved fairy atop it. Gold-plated mirrors or paintings filled empty wall spots.

The dining room sat only fifty, but the outside patio could accommodate another hundred if the weather allowed. For larger events, tents could be set up on the lawn.

After their coffee was poured, Jean and Thomas disappeared.

"When it's just me, I let Chef Alice make whatever she wants." He smiled. "So far, she's never steered me wrong."

"I could eat a horse," Robin said with a groan. "I think with everything that happened last night"—he noticed her shiver— "I ran through my carbs from dinner."

"Yeah," he agreed.

"Besides, we'll want to stock up since I plan on seeing every single inch of this place, inside and out." She leaned her elbows on the table and lowered her voice. "Tell me there are secret passages. Please, let there be secret passages."

He chuckled and mimicked her by placing his elbows on the table and lowering his voice. "A few."

Breakfast was one of his favorites—varied local cheeses, meats, and eggs, and, of course, freshly made croissants, which he dribbled some of the château's honey over.

"You guys make your own honey?" Robin asked after she bit into her croissant. "Yum." She groaned with pleasure.

"Honey and jams from the fruit trees, along with eggs and beef. The château used to be one of the biggest suppliers of produce in the area. Now, most everything is retained for the big events, and what isn't used, they sell. The proceeds go to a local charity for the children's hospital. My mother was the one that came up with that part. In the past, the owner of the château kept all the proceeds."

"And the workers?" she asked as she sipped on her coffee.

"They all get paid for their time." He smiled. "Most of them throw in extra time since the charity is something dear to their hearts. One of our staff, Michel, who works in the kitchen, his son was pretty sick a few years back. If it wasn't for the hospital and the donations... he wouldn't have just had his tenth birthday."

"How wonderful." She smiled and then glanced around. "I can just imagine this place packed with men in suits and women in long flowing dresses." She sighed.

"You won't have to imagine for long. Marcus has requested that there be a ball set up for your shooting."

"Right." She smiled. "You should see my dress for the dream sequence." She practically squealed. "Not to mention the dress for the ball. It's where I— I mean my character, Meg—meets the love of her life, Roger."

"Tom Levi?" he asked, trying to ignore the flames of jealousy.

"Yes," Robin answered.

"Hold up, you're shooting the scene where you are supposed to see each other for the first time? Haven't you been filming for months now?" he asked, a little confused.

"Yes." She chuckled. "I'll tell you all about the wonders of filmmaking while you show me around." She lowered her voice. "And the secret passages."

"Right." He nodded to Jean that they were done.

He figured he'd start the tour from the bottom floor since he'd planned a surprise lunch on the top of his tower, overlooking the property, before they headed out for a ride to show her the grounds.

While they went room by room in the guest chambers, she talked about how filming happened. She told him about her experiences on each movie that she'd done and how much fun it was changing into other people.

The lower floors had plenty of narrow passages for them to explore. He introduced her to the kitchen staff who were on hand at the moment. He showed her everything on the lower floors that he could, but many of the rooms were private on the east side, so he kept to the main working areas like the kitchens, the prep rooms, laundry, and a large dining room for staff members.

"This"—he motioned to a painting— "is our first hidden passage." He wiggled his eyes.

"Oh!" Robin's eyes lit up.

He leaned against the wall and crossed his arms. "Think you can figure out how it opens?"

CHAPTER NINE

Robin narrowed her eyes and looked at the painting of a man holding up a dead turkey. The man's leg was propped casually up on a stool and he had a gun slung over his shoulder.

She ran her fingers over the picture frame, but she grew frustrated when she didn't find any levers or buttons. Then she ran her eyes over the image and narrowed them as she leaned closer to get a better look. There was something odd about the top button of the man's shirt. She hovered her hand over it. She glanced at Blake in question, and he nodded his encouragement. She touched the man's top silver button and gasped and jumped back when the entire paneled wall, painting included, slid back silently.

"Oh my god. That was amazing." She turned to Blake, then looked inside at the narrow circular staircase. "Where does it go?"

"To each floor. It's a servant's staircase."

"Then why hide it?" She started up the stairs, dipping her head so she wouldn't bump it. It was very narrow. She doubted anyone carrying anything would be able to make it up or down without spilling.

"Because servants are not to be seen," Blake said sarcastically. "Or so the wealthy way back in the nineteenth century thought."

"Some still think that way," she said over her shoulder as he followed her up. If she'd thought she'd had a difficult time, seeing him hunched over had her laughing. "Is the exit hidden too?" she asked, stopping at the top of the stairs.

"From the inside, no." He pushed the wall and it slid open.

They stepped out into the hallway, just outside the main hall. When the wall closed, she turned around and laughed when she saw the same painting that had been downstairs, only this time the man held up two pheasants. Instantly, she noticed the change and understood its meaning.

"Same image, but two dead animals. Tell me there are three on the top floor?" she asked.

He smiled. "Three ducks."

"Unique." She smiled. "How did I not see this painting before?" She looked at the image, then looked around. They must have passed by here at least twice before now.

"It's forgettable." He shrugged. "Compared to the rest of the property."

"True." She looked at the rest of the hallway, then back at the painting. "Yet it doesn't look out of place. Are the rest of the hidden passages behind paintings?"

"No. The library entrance, remember?" he said walking down the hallway.

"Right. How many more are there?" she asked eagerly.

He chuckled. "On this floor..." He stopped and thought about it. "Two. On the upper floors, there are a few more.

Mostly so the chambermaids could move around without being seen."

They stepped into the next room. "The morning room," he said, motioning around.

The white and gold room was directly out of every historical movie she'd ever seen. A massive gold-plated deer-antler chandelier hung over white frail-looking sofas that faced one another. Gold and marble end tables held statues while gold-framed pictures hung on gold wires from the walls.

"Wow, someone sure liked gold," she said, turning in circles.

He chuckled. "It never goes out of style. Or so I'm told."

"Right." She smiled. "What's through here?"

"The drawing rooms. Apparently, women would retire there after spending their morning sipping tea or whatever in here," he said as they moved into a cozier room decorated in soft blue.

"Where's the ballroom?" she asked, turning in circles and trying to take everything in.

"That's next on the tour." He took her hand and they walked through an archway that led them back out into a different hallway. They passed through another smaller sitting room, which he just called the smoke room. She assumed it was because men would retire there to smoke since it was decorated very masculinely with a bunch of hunting trophies and darker colors. Then they stepped into another hallway, and she noticed the massive doors, four of them, two on either side of a huge painting with a couple in nineteenth-century formal attire.

"Who are they?" she asked, stopping in front of the painting.

"Monique and Claude de Beauvoir." He took her hand

and pulled her into the massive ballroom. Two huge chandeliers hung over the perfect wood floor. The pale blue walls were covered with large scenic paintings or mirrors framed with gold. Archways with French doors led out to the veranda with the view of the perfectly manicured grounds beyond. "The de Beauvoirs were the first to inhabit the château. Claude built the property for Monique as a wedding gift. However, construction finished and the very next year Monique died in childbirth giving Claude his only child." Blake paused and wiggled his eyebrows. "A daughter."

"The horror." She gasped, going along with him. "No heir to take his fortune?"

Blake chuckled. "Can you believe some families still think that way?" He rolled his eyes.

"The fact that daughters aren't seen as being on the same level as sons is a mystery," she said, remembering her father struggling with wanting a son instead of two daughters.

"If it were me, I would have doted on my daughter even more. Especially after my wife, presumably the love of my life, had died giving her life." Blake took her hand and spun her around on the floor.

She arched her eyebrows. "You dance too?"

He chuckled. "You don't spend a few weeks each summer living in a place with its own ballroom and not learn. Plus, my mother insisted it would get me all the girls." He winked and then expertly spun her around, making her laugh.

"A man of many talents," she said after he pulled her close. She rested her head on his shoulder.

"From what I've read in a few articles, you have a few

hidden talents too. Was it gymnastics or ballet?" he asked, looking down at her.

She laughed. "Neither. Tap." She smiled and then with her hiking boots, tapped a simple combination and ended the move with a spin, causing him to laugh. "Okay, hiking boots don't do the move justice."

"I don't know, I'm impressed." He clapped for her.

"Show me more of this place." She motioned to the next archway.

For the next hour, she got lost in all the rooms on the main level. Besides the morning, drawing, and smoking rooms, there were sitting rooms, music rooms, and even a parlor, where guests were entertained while waiting to be shown to the sitting, music, or parlor rooms.

They moved past the main hall, where she stopped briefly to glance around once more before heading up the east marble staircase. This one was almost as elaborate as the main circular staircase.

"My family's rooms are down to the right." He motioned once they reached the top of the stairs. "To the left..." He took her hand and led her down the opposite hallway. "The hidden servants' staircase." He motioned to the same painting, where the man was holding three dead ducks. They walked past the wall, and there was another set of narrow stairs a few feet away.

"Tell me employees use these instead of the narrow circular one," she said as they turned down another hallway.

"Yes, the hidden stairs are far too small. I guess servants used to be midgets or children." He shook his head. "Honestly, I think we are the first ones to use them in years." He shrugged. "This is the upper meeting room. They're used for bridal parties, pictures, and so on." He opened a heavy wood door to another sitting room. "There are three smaller changing rooms." He motioned to the doorways. "Bathrooms and such." They continued down the hallway.

"Did you have the run of this place growing up?" she asked as they passed by another group of guest rooms, which he explained were rented out for parties.

"Yes. Well, except during my high school years. A few times when we were here, there were events that couldn't be cancelled. A few times there were guests running around while we were here. Which made staying here a little more fun" He shrugged.

"But you block out the calendar now when you visit?" she asked as they passed by even more bedrooms.

"Yeah. My brother-in-law takes my security very seriously. After I became a senator, he persuaded the family to make the change."

She stopped after the tenth bedroom. They were beginning to all look alike. Each one was pretty enough with their unique decorations, but she wanted to see the secret passages.

"Where are the passages?" she asked, looking around.

Blake smiled. "Here." He stepped around a corner and walked to the end of the shorter hallway. He pushed in the wall, much like he had to gain access to the library.

"Each wall at the end of the short hallways opens up to another long hallway going down between all of the guest rooms. They're joined at the back to another wider staircase." He motioned for her to step inside. "We'll go up instead of down when we reach the end."

The hallway was a lot narrower than any of the ones they'd used before now. Not too narrow that someone carrying a tray of food or a basket of laundry couldn't pass through, but narrow enough that Blake had to walk behind her as she went.

The hallway forked many times, but finally they reached another circular staircase. This one was double the width of the first one.

"Aren't we on the top floor?" she asked, frowning as she looked up the staircase.

"Head on up and see for yourself." He motioned.

As she started to climb, the round staircase straightened out. By the time she reached the top, she realized they were at one of the corner towers.

"Wow," she said, stepping into the very square sitting room. There was a comfortable sofa and chair with a book-shelf and a small desk area. "Are all four of the towers the same?"

"Yes and no. The ones over the west wing are set up for photo shoots for weddings or events. The other east tower is my parents' private spot. This one is all mine." He smiled. "I come up here when I visit and work a lot of times."

"It's nice." She walked over and looked out the window. "Wow, that view." She looked over the garden area and could just see the road leading into the château as well as the stables and parking area.

"From this side, you can see the lake," Blake suggested. She moved over to the next window and smiled. "Nice. Is all that land yours too?"

"Most of it. Beyond the lake was donated to the region for a game preserve. There's more." He motioned towards another set of stairs.

She glanced up at them. There was a glass door at the top, and she could see the sunlight shining in it.

"Go on." He smiled and took her hand.

When they stepped out onto the roof of the tower, she noticed the picnic setup. A basket of food sat on a large blanket in the middle of the railed-in area. A bottle of champagne sat chilling in a silver bucket.

Blake walked over and motioned for her to sit as he picked up the bottle and opened it, then poured them each a glass.

"When did you arrange all of this?" she asked when he handed her the glass.

"While you were drying your hair." He sat next to her. "I figured you'd enjoy the view while we had cold sandwiches."

She smiled and tapped her glass to his. "You figured right."

CHAPTER TEN

Somehow, showing Robin around the château was like showing her a part of his childhood. Each time she discovered a new room, he grew excited and amazed at the surroundings with her. It was like seeing the château for the first time again.

They spent more than an hour up on the roof patio, enjoying the sights and the food the kitchen had prepared for them. Afterward, they headed down to the ground floor and stepped out on the large veranda to start making their way around the grounds. He'd spent a lot of his youth inside the château since his mother had been very protective after the kidnapping. But still, the grounds were as familiar to him as the inside.

The stables were near the front and on the west side of the property. There were large, fenced pastures for the horses to roam when not in one of the many luxurious stalls. The sound of horses' hooves echoed from the stable's cobblestone flooring as they were led out to the mounting blocks for them.

He had his favorite mount, a white gelding by the name

of Tinkerbell. Robin laughed at the name until she was introduced to her horse, Sugar Plum.

"See the theme there?" he joked as he helped her up onto her gelding's back.

"It's nice," she said once he was seated. "I bet the guests adore the theme. I noticed it throughout the house. I thought those were cherubs on the ceiling paintings and carvings throughout until I looked a little closer. They're fairies."

"There are two hundred and twelve unique fairies in the château, including paintings, carvings, and statues." He smiled as they started walking the horses from the stables. "I counted once."

"You must have had a lot of time on your hands."

"It kept my mind off... things," he admitted, unsure why he felt the need to talk to her about his childhood now. Maybe because he was on the back of a horse again? How long had it been since he'd ridden?

"I bet it was difficult, coming back from something like that. I'm having a time of it just replaying what happened last night," she said with a sigh as she glanced around.

"Last night was... scary," he admitted. "You are okay?"

"Yes." She smiled over at him. "Just as long as you are."

"I am. I was back then too. Of course, as an eight-year-old, it took me a lot longer to be... okay."

"This place probably helped a lot." She glanced around. "It's gorgeous."

They had ridden the path towards the lake, and he figured they'd ride around it and maybe stop on the other side, to see the château from across the still waters.

"Yes, it did help. I think that's why my parents went through the hassle of getting this place a few years after the kidnapping. Everything in the States was... well, chaotic.

My face was plastered on every magazine or newspaper. We couldn't turn on the television without seeing the story." He remembered the first time he'd seen his scarred face on the television set. The still image had been taken when Ethan had been carrying him up the drive as his mother and father had rushed out to get him back. The pure joy on his parents' faces had been obvious to all. "Coming to France had just been luck. As I said, my dad knew a guy who knew the previous owners. He sunk everything he had into the place. For a while, we lived in a little apartment back in the States so we could fix this place up. Then money started flowing in from renting the château out and a few of my father's investments paid off and they purchased the home they're in now."

"I hadn't heard of your family's financial struggles during that time," she said, looking slightly concerned.

"They weren't struggles. Not by any real standards. A lot of others have had it worse. But it was made clear that my parents would do anything and everything they could to protect me and help me through the difficult time." He smiled and pulled Tinkerbell to a stop. He'd been talking nonstop since they'd left the stables. "Let's stop here for a while," he suggested. "There's a large rock that hangs over the water. It's a perfect spot to sit in the sun. We can let the horses graze."

"That sounds amazing." She sighed. "I'd forgotten how much horseback riding stiffens your backside." She slid off her mount effortlessly, then rubbed her butt slightly as she chuckled.

He slid off his horse and took her reins and his and tied them around a tree branch. He grabbed the blanket from the saddlebag and took her hand and walked through the tall grass to the water's edge.

"This spot is beautiful," she said once they were sitting on the blanket in the shade of a large oak.

"One of my favorites. I have a small pond on my property in Georgia. It's nothing like this, but it reminds me of here."

"If I lean out my balcony at my apartment in Santa Barbara, I can see the ocean," she said with a smile.

"I would have thought that a big star like you"—he nudged her shoulder playfully— "would have one of those McMansions."

She chuckled. "Not on your life. I'm gone months at a time filming. I don't even want to care for a houseplant let alone an entire house." She turned and looked at him. "What about you? Your place, if I remember correctly, is huge."

"It's a barndominium." He smiled.

"A..." She shook her head. "I've seen pictures, but why is it called a barndominium?"

He laughed. "You start with an old barn. Something classic looking."

"Like the red one in all the Superman movies?" she asked.

He laughed again. "Exactly. Mine was gray when I purchased it. Then, you turn it into a home." He pulled out his phone and flipped through his pictures. "Here, see." He showed her the image of his home. "Garage space for four cars, a huge covered porch out front, a massive back deck, four bedrooms, four baths, and more than four thousand square feet of living space. Not to mention all the land that goes with it."

"It looks amazing. What do you do with all that space?" she asked as she handed him back his phone.

He shrugged and tucked his phone away. "Work, play,

host guests and family. And I have as much privacy as I want. It's Georgia, not California or DC. I stay at my dad's condo when I'm needed there."

"Sounds like you enjoy country living, here and at home." She sighed. "I grew up in a small town and thought I'd grown tired of it. But after a few years of being in the city, I'm missing it." She looked around. "The fresh air, the..." She glanced at him. "Privacy."

"As you said, you can live wherever. Why not get a place somewhere you can enjoy?"

"I've thought about it. Heading back to Castle Rock just seemed..." She dropped off.

"Like a failure?" he suggested.

She nodded. "How did you guess?"

He shrugged. "I live within ten miles of where I was born. Not a lot of people stick around those parts. I struggled with returning after my college years. Thought the same thing, that somehow returning home was taboo. Then I went into politics and nothing else mattered. Seeing the changes I've helped push through, the people that have benefited from my work, that's what mattered." He picked up her hand and ran his thumb across her palm. "You bring joy to people. Let them forget their troubles for a few hours. Make them fall in love with you, or, in the case of your movie *Alone*"—he shivered— "be scared of you."

She laughed. "I was scared of myself after that. I think it's why I like romance and action films instead."

"You're good at it. Convincing others you're someone else."

"Some say the same about you." She tilted her head as her eyes ran over him. "You're nothing like how the press portrays you."

He relaxed back and pulled her against his chest. She leaned against him as they sat facing the water.

"I am the person I have to be to get things done. I'm sure you are the same. We portray what they need to see in order to sell or convince others to buy into us." He sighed as he watched a few dragonflies flying over the top of the water while he thought about all the meetings he was missing. Not that he was concerned he was missing something. Actually, he was thankful. Negotiations were going well, and he wasn't going to be missed since he'd had his say the first few days.

"Does it get old for you?" she asked, breaking into his thoughts.

"No. You?" He glanced down at her.

"No. If it ever did, I could always take a break. Maybe go back to television?" She rested her head against his chest. "Get married, have kids, maybe build my very own barn-dominium."

"You'd know who to call for advice." He smiled. "You're always welcome to come to check out my place, for ideas."

She sat up and turned towards him. Her eyes searched his. "I'd like that. I'm not doing anything after filming stops."

His eyebrows shot up for a split second, then he pulled her against his chest and kissed her. Her body was plastered to his as he poured everything he was feeling into the kiss. She buried her fingers in his hair.

"Just how private is this land?" she asked between kisses.

For an answer, he pulled her down on top of him and started removing her shirt. He could tell she had lost patience and sat up to pull her shirt over her head. When she reached for the clasp of her jeans, he stopped her.

"Here, let me." He changed their positions until she lay flat on the blanket, looking up at him.

His gaze traveled over her, taking in her crisp white bra, her perfect toned and tanned skin. Her long braid lay over her shoulder and her amber eyes turned a darker shade when he ran his fingertips over her belly button, down to slowly unsnap her jeans. Sliding them down her rounded hips, he smiled.

"I'm so thankful for your curves." He cupped her hip and watched her eyes close.

"I refuse to work with anyone who says I need to lose weight," she said softly. She gasped when his fingers dipped under her jeans to play over her panties.

"Blake." Robin gripped his wrist, trying to get him to move quicker.

"The way the sunlight hits your skin," he said, keeping his movements slow. "It's mesmerizing." He dipped his head down and sampled the taste of her skin between her breasts.

"I need you." Robin started pulling off his shirt. He let her and even sat back and helped remove it, only to return to his slow torture of running his lips over her bare skin.

When he dipped a finger under the silk covering her, she arched and cried out as her nails dug into his shoulders.

"I can't wait for you," she moaned.

"Don't wait," he begged before he covered her sex with his mouth. The moment he felt her convulse under him was the moment he knew that he wanted to have her in his life.

She surprised him by rolling over on top of him, her mouth sliding down his neck, his chest, to just above the button of his jeans.

"My turn." She smiled up at him while her fingers worked to unclasp his jeans, then slide them down until he was freed. When she took him into her mouth, his eyes crossed, and he lost himself completely.

"I've never done that outside before," she said a while later as they lay, fully clothed again, looking up at the leaves of the trees and the white fluffy clouds that drifted above.

"Me either," he admitted. "It was…"

"Exuberating," she said with a giggle.

He smiled. "I never thought that I'd be that into… the outdoors so much," he joked.

She poked a finger into his ribs. "Done gloating?" she asked, sitting up.

"Not gloating." He sat up with her. "Just appreciating… nature."

She laughed. "For some reason, I'm starving again."

"Dinner will be waiting for us." He stood up, then pulled her up into his arms and kissed her. "This feels right," he said, looking into her eyes. "Here, with you like this."

She nodded. "It does."

"You weren't joking earlier? You'll come back to my place once filming is done?" he asked, a little afraid that she'd back out.

"I wasn't joking. If you'll have me, I'd love to see your home." She lifted on her toes and kissed him again.

On the ride back to the stables he was riding on air. He was already making plans in his mind. Moving his calendar around so that he would have as much time as possible with her.

He wanted whatever time he had with her to be perfect. As with all of his relationships in the past, he knew that his work would most likely get in the way soon enough. But until then, he was going to enjoy being with Robin, for as long as she would have him.

When they returned to the château, they were met by his brother-in-law Ethan and Javan.

He gave both men hugs and then introduced them to Robin. He didn't think it was possible for Javan to blush, but when the large Jamaican asked for a selfie with Robin, he could have sworn the man's cheeks turned a bright red.

One thing was clear. With both of the men staying at the château, he felt as if he could finally relax just knowing that Robin would be safe.

CHAPTER ELEVEN

Sitting in the library, a blanket over her lap and a cup of hot tea with little berry cakes in front of her, she figured she'd died and gone to heaven. She'd just finished the book she'd been trying to read in Paris and was now looking around the massive room. Blake's head was buried in his book as he sat next to her.

"Bored already?" he asked, glancing up from his pages.

While she'd picked a light romantic read, he'd chosen an action-packed murder mystery. Not that she didn't occasionally love a good mystery, but while in Paris, she'd stuck to lighthearted reading.

Now, however, she wanted something juicier.

"No, just done." She set her book down. "Where would I look for something a little more... exciting?"

He glanced down at the cover of her book and the half-naked man on the cover and laughed. "That wasn't exciting?"

She smiled. "Thrilling, then."

"Mystery?" he asked. When she nodded, he motioned

to the corner of the library. "There are some Tom Clancy novels."

She frowned. "I've read most of his already."

Blake's eyebrows rose. Then he tilted his head. "Mary Higgins Clark?"

She nodded. "Love her, but I'm in the mood for something... older."

He smiled. "Agatha Christie?"

She nodded. "Would love to. I've always wanted to read a few of hers I never got to."

"Which ones?" he asked, setting his book down.

She thought about it. "*Death on the Nile, Endless Night,* or *The Pale Horse.*"

"We have all three." He stood up, took her hand, and walked over to the corner with her. "The mystery section." He waved to the large bookshelves that filled the corner. "Takes up this entire corner. Books are alphabetical by author's last name."

"Just like in a bookstore." She smiled.

"My mother's doing. She says that any respectable reader knows how to organize her books," Blake said with a chuckle. "It took us three weeks one summer to rearrange this entire collection." He motioned to the room.

"You and your mother arranged all of these?" She took down a copy of *Death on the Nile* and began reading the back cover.

"Us and a few staff members." He shrugged. "We donated more than three hundred titles to the local library once we were done. We even found a few classics that were worth a lot of money. My father auctioned them off to help pay for some of the woodwork that needed repairing in here." He motioned to the stairs and the walls. "Not to mention the electric wiring. Anyway..." He nodded to the book. "I wouldn't think that after the other night you would want something so dark?"

"It's Agatha Christie." She shrugged. "A different kind of dark." She followed him back over to the sofa and sat down next to him. She popped a small fruit into her mouth, then took a sip of her tea.

Within half an hour, she was plastered against Blake's side as she continued reading quickly. She'd wrapped the blanket around them both and felt every fiber of her being on alert.

"Are you okay?" Blake asked, glancing down at her.

"Yes, no." She frowned and glanced around the room, suddenly seeing every dark corner, every shadow that danced with the dim light. "It's so..." She glanced back at the book. "I can't put it down."

He chuckled, the sound reverberating in her soul. "Okay, don't then. Would you like some fresh tea?"

"No." She almost jumped. "Don't leave."

"I wasn't going to. I can have it delivered up here," he suggested.

"Oh." She relaxed slightly. "Okay, maybe... some more of those cakes?"

He nodded and moved to get up. Her hand wrapped around his arm. "I need to call." He motioned to the phone on the desk. His smug smile made her realize she was being stupid.

She tried to relax and tell herself it was just a story, but the fact was, she had always gotten too into books. It was the main reason she loved acting. Helping others to experience the stories the way she did in her head was her life's goal.

She was so involved in reading, that she didn't even register when the fresh tea and cakes arrived. When Blake offered her one, she took it and shoved it in her mouth as she turned a page.

"Do you always get this into a book?" he asked her as he handed her the tea.

"Yes," she said, taking the cup and continuing to read.

When she finished the book, he was leaning back on the sofa, his eyes closed as she rested against him.

"Finished?" he asked, coming awake.

"Yes." She sighed. "Wow, that woman knew how to write a great story."

"You're a speed reader," he said, shifting.

"Didn't you finish your book?" she asked, looking at his book on the table.

"Yes, but I started it a few weeks ago. You started that one..." He glanced at his watch and winced. "Four hours ago."

She stretched her arms over her head and then snuggled against his chest. "It helps when reading through scripts."

"Did you enjoy the story?" he asked.

"So much so." She closed her eyes, suddenly feeling tired.

"Tired?" he asked in a soothing tone.

"So much so." She yawned.

She gasped when he quickly stood up, swooped her up into his arms, and started carrying her from the room.

"This is new too." She smiled and snuggled into his chest.

"Being carried?"

"Hmm," she agreed with a nod. "When I was filming *Magnanimous*, Clark Stevens had to carry me after I'd been shot in a scene, but since he couldn't lift me, I had to be on wires." She yawned again.

Blake stopped in the hallway and looked down at her.

"Clark Stevens couldn't lift you?" He shifted her and then smiled. "You're light as a feather."

She laughed. "You lie like a politician."

He laughed and continued walking. "I thought Clark had all those muscles?"

"Hollywood magic," she said. "He has some, but not as much as he wants everyone to think."

"Apparently not, if he can't lift a hundred pounds," Blake said, taking the stairs two at a time. When they reached the top, she noticed that he wasn't even winded.

"Okay, that was impressive." She felt more awake now. "Plus, I weigh more than a hundred pounds."

He smiled down at her. "One of those rooms in my barndominium is a home gym," he said with a shrug as he continued down the hallway towards his rooms.

"I like it here." She glanced around as he continued walking. "It's quiet." She wanted to tell him that she liked it so much because of him, but instead rested her head on his shoulder again.

"Wait until filming starts. There'll be plenty of noise." He stepped into his rooms and set her down on the edge of the bed. Then he knelt and started removing her shoes.

"Is this part of the turn-down service?" she joked.

He glanced up at her and smiled. Just that smile had her knees going weak. She'd never had a man affect her like Blake did. He turned her brain into mush, and her insides buzzed as if electricity was pulsing through her.

She thought he was going to crawl in the bed with her, make love to her all night. Instead, he crawled in, pulled her against his chest, and buried his face in her hair.

"Thank you for today," he said softly. She listened while his breathing leveled, and he fell asleep.

Smiling, she allowed herself to drift off.

Someone was chasing her. It was too dark to see who, but she knew, in her sleepy mind, that she had to get away. She had to run. Only, her legs wouldn't work the way she knew they could. Instead of the face pace she used on the treadmill in the gym, she moved slowly, as if she were running in quicksand. Her feet felt like lead weights, holding her back.

They were closing on her. Soon, she'd feel the icy fingers of death grip her throat. Gasping for breath, fighting the sludge, she cried out.

"Robin!" Blake's soothing voice shook her from the nightmare. His warm strong arms wrapped around her chilled body. She couldn't stop the shaking as she held onto him while he soothed her.

"Sorry," she said, allowing the tears to soak his bare chest.

"I've got you." He kissed her forehead. Then his arms grew tighter until she was once more gasping for air. "And I'm never going to let you go." She cried out and tried to fight his hold.

"Robin!" Blake's scream broke her from the dream within the dream. His hands rested on her shoulders as he shook her awake.

The lights were on, bathing the room in soft light, allowing her to see his worried look.

She jumped out of bed and wrapped her arms around herself. She paced to the window as she gulped for air.

"Are you okay?" Blake asked, concern lacing his voice.

The fact that he didn't rush to her and wrap his arms around her soothed her and made her feel like an idiot for the dream.

"Yes." She sighed as her heart settled in her chest, and she turned towards him. He was sitting on the edge of the bed, holding out a blanket for her. Walking over, she took it and wrapped it around herself.

"Want to talk about it?" he asked, shifting slightly, giving her plenty of room to sit down.

"It was a dream inside a dream." She sat down and, since she wanted to prove to herself that he wasn't the monster he'd been in her head, she leaned against his shoulder. "Someone was chasing me. You know, the kind of dream where nothing works on your body, dragging you down?"

"Yeah." He gently laid a hand over her shoulder. "Then?"

"Then, you woke me, and everything was okay until it wasn't." She shivered slightly.

"I was the bad guy?" he asked softly.

"Yes and no." She closed her eyes. "I don't know what's what anymore. I think the book twisted my mind," she said with a nervous chuckle.

"Hey." He nudged her until she looked up into his eyes. "I get it. After..." He took a few deep breaths. "After the kidnapping, I had all sorts of crazy dreams. Ones where my parents' faces replaced the faces of my kidnappers. For weeks." He shook his head slightly. "Months actually. I was afraid of my father and mother. Even my sister. Ann was in on the kidnapping in my mind."

"I don't think you're smothering me," she said and watched his eyebrows shoot up. "I mean..." She shook her head. "I know it's just..."

"Hey," he said, lifting his hand to brush a finger across her cheek. "I get it. This is all moving so quickly." He nodded slightly. "I guess we've allowed ourselves to project things forward because of our feelings. If you need time—"

"No," she broke in. "As you said, I think it's... all just a little much with the shooting." She chuckled. "I shouldn't have read Agatha Christie."

He smiled at her. "Feel better now that you've talked about it?"

"Yes," she said after she assessed herself.

"Need something to drink?"

"Water," she said, shifting to stand up and get it herself.

"No, you stay here. I'll get it." He walked to the bathroom and brought back a glass of water for her.

She drank a few sips and felt more settled.

"Better?"

She nodded. "Thank you."

He pulled her against his chest on the bed and turned off the light. She listened to his breathing and relaxed even more.

"If you want, there are plenty of rooms..." he started, but she stopped him by leaning up and kissing him.

"I'm right where I want to be." She rested back against him. "Even if my mind twists what we have between us." She sighed. "I trust you. Completely."

CHAPTER TWELVE

By the time the film crew showed up, Blake was positive that he had completely lost his heart to Robin. He'd never spent a more perfect two days in his life. Even when the clouds and rain detoured their outdoor activities to inside on their second day together.

Robin was everything he'd ever dreamed of. She was smart, funny, and those legs of hers...

He glanced over to the yoga pants she was wearing as she helped unload boxes with the rest of the crew. The fact that she was an A-lister and still got her hands dirty unloading lights made him realize just how perfect she was. He'd never met anyone as down to earth as she was in the industry.

"Where do you want these?" he asked Marcus as he shifted the box in his hands.

For the past four hours, he'd been showing the entire crew around the château and then unloading the four large truckloads of equipment.

Marcus and a few other crew members had decided that the majority of filming would happen in the ballroom, the main hall, and the grand staircase. Which meant most of the equipment was being stored in the sitting rooms next to the main hall and ballroom.

"Those can go in with the others," Marcus answered. As Blake moved to take them, Marcus joined him. "How's she doing?" he asked in a low tone.

Blake glanced over to Robin, who was laughing with her stylist and her husband.

"Good." He shrugged. "She's had a few nightmares, but so far…"

"She looks happier than when I saw her last," Marcus said, opening the door for Blake. He shifted the heavy box and stepped inside.

"Yeah, thanks for giving her time off. We appreciated it," Blake said.

"We think we know what happened. Amanda Hughes and I had a chat. For the past year, Robin's been getting… threats." Blake stopped walking to look at Marcus.

"What kind of threats?" he asked, feeling his gut twist.

Marcus glanced around. "The credible kind. It's why Amanda's on a plane right now heading here."

He thought about telling Ethan and Javan about the threats. They had set up security in his sister's room, down the hall from their own.

"Do you think that's who broke into her trailer? The person who shot at us?" he asked.

Marcus shrugged. "The police are looking into it. We don't have a name. Otherwise, there would be an arrest."

"This has been going on for a year?" he asked, setting down the box finally.

"Yeah. According to Amanda, she's had people looking into the threatening messages," Marcus added.

"Letters? Emails?" he asked, thinking of the threats he'd gotten most of his life.

"Both, as well as some phone calls. Both Robin and Amanda have had to change their numbers a few times," Marcus answered.

"Robin has known about them?" he asked, wondering why she hadn't mentioned the threats to him.

"No, Amanda made that part clear. She's paid to worry for Robin. All Robin has known is that she had to change her number." Marcus nodded. "It's her job to shoulder the concern and protect her client. When Robin's in the States, she has a security detail. Since she was on set in Paris, Amanda arranged to make sure we had our security detail." Marcus sighed. "Which I guess we failed at." He glanced around. "I've hired a crew..."

"You didn't need to bother. I've got my brother-in-law and his detail watching Robin." Blake motioned towards the doors where he knew Javan was watching Robin. "I'll intro-duce you later."

Marcus smiled. "I think I met them. We are talking tall, dark, and very Jamaican?"

Blake chuckled. "Yes, and he's married." Then he frowned. "And aren't you as well?"

"Happily." Marcus smiled. "Ramon is the love of my life." He glanced down at his wedding band. "But I'm not dead." He chuckled. "Either way, I'm happy that Robin seems more relaxed. I think the fresh country air helped out. Not to mention enjoying this beautiful place." He glanced around the hall. "We are lucky the two of you bumped into one another the other night. We were having a hell of a time finding a place for filming after the cancelation."

"It's the least I could do. Besides, it can only help the

tourism to keep this place rented out," he admitted. "The last time someone filmed here, we were booked solid for two years."

They were laughing and joking when they stepped back outside as Robin was heading in. She took his hand and pulled him inside the door with her.

"Everything okay?" he asked her, but as an answer, she pulled up on her toes and kissed him.

"Yes, everything is perfect." She smiled up at him. "Thank you for this."

His hands moved to her hips. "For the kiss? Any time," he joked.

She chuckled and kissed him again. "Everyone is saying how perfect this place is. The only thing that is missing is snow since the ball is supposed to be taking place on New Year's. But thanks to the magic of Hollywood..." She dropped off. "We'll have snow. Most of these boxes we've been unloading are decorations."

"I've never watched a movie being made. This should be fun." He pulled her a little closer, enjoying the soft scent of flowers that always seemed to follow her.

"Marcus was building up the courage to ask you to be an extra," Robin said with a smile.

"Oh?" He thought about it. How many interviews had he done in his life? Too many to count. He was comfortable in front of a camera. Of course, it hadn't always been that way. Now, however, he no longer felt sick to his stomach each time he stepped in front of the lens. "I might be persuaded."

She took his hand and walked further into the hallway. "For now, let's get out of everyone's way." She continued to head towards the staircase, pulling him along.

"Don't they need our help?" he asked, glancing over his

shoulder.

"No, now that everything's unloaded, we'll just be in the way. Filming starts later tonight, and I need to rest since we'll probably work all night long." The look she gave him over her shoulder had his heart skipping.

"I could rest," he said with a smile. He started walking faster, causing her to chuckle.

Lying in bed with Robin's head resting on his bare chest was one of the best feelings in the world. Even though she was fast asleep, he continued to stare up at the ceiling and think.

He tried not to worry about what Marcus had said. How someone had been threatening Robin for over a year. He knew that a lot of Hollywood actors had stalkers and remembered a few horror stories when those stalkers had hurt or, in a few cases, killed.

But the fact that Robin was oblivious to it somehow pissed him off. If it was him, he would want to know. After what he'd been through as a child, he knew full well that there were monsters in the darkness. It helped him to be less... trusting.

Before he'd been nabbed that day, he would have easily talked to any stranger that was kind or asserted authority. Then again, he'd been eight. After that, however, his trust had disappeared. He'd even demanded proof his teacher worked for the school that next year after his return.

Thankfully, Ms. Nelson had been kind enough to present him with her school ID. Later, he'd found out that all his teachers had gone out of their way to make him feel comfortable.

Was that what Robin's agent was doing? Keeping Robin in the dark so she didn't worry?

He remembered the nightmare she'd had a couple of

nights ago and frowned.

In the past few days, she'd shown him how strong of a person she was. Nightmares were part of the healing process, as he'd found out long ago. It was your subconscious trying to make sense of the horrors you'd gone through. But since that night, Robin hadn't mentioned any more scary dreams.

They had talked about what had happened thoroughly. They had even come to an understanding that it could have been either of them someone was aiming at or trying to scare.

He lost track of time thinking and jumped slightly when Robin's cell phone alarm chimed and woke her.

"Did you rest?" she asked, stretching her arms over her head. The sight of her bare breasts had him smiling.

"Enough. You?" he asked, cupping her.

She moaned and rolled towards him. "Enough," she said, kissing him. "Make love to me," she said. He rolled her over and complied.

Pleasing her was something he figured he could do for years to come without fail. She responded so much to his touch and he to hers. Yet there was another connection they had that hadn't been there with anyone else he'd been with before.

When they stepped into the shower almost half an hour later, he held onto her as the warm water washed over them both.

"What happens now?" he asked.

She sighed. "Now it's hair and makeup, then costume. Then we'll run over lines while we work out where filming will take place." She glanced up at him. "Will you be able to watch?"

He nodded. "I have a virtual meeting around three. I'll

have to sneak away for that. But after that, I'm curious to see the process. Will it make you nervous to have me there?"

She smiled up at him as she ran her hands over his shoulders. "When I'm in character, I don't even know the camera is there."

He kissed her. "Then you're lucky. When I get interviewed, I can't stop thinking about it."

"It's a lot different when you're portraying yourself," she admitted. "When I have to become someone else"—she shrugged and started washing her long hair— "I put Robin Stein on a shelf and become my character."

"It must be nice," he admitted, thinking about all the years long ago when he'd dreamed of disappearing. Those years he'd been hunted down by the press for an interview about what he'd gone through as an eight-year-old child.

"It can be." She rinsed her hair. "Claire says it was my way of coping."

"Coping?" he asked, and she stilled, her eyes searching his.

"Our parents... weren't perfect." She shook her head and dropped her hands to her side. "Later?"

He nodded. "For now, what do you need from me to help you get ready?" He handed her the large bottle of conditioner she'd brought into his shower a few days ago.

Smiling, she took it and dumped some into her hand, and started lathering her hair.

"I'll spend about an hour in hair and makeup before we start shooting," She shrugged. "Sit back and enjoy the show."

Which is exactly what he did for the next two hours.

He met Amanda Hughes, Robin's agent. Seeing how easily the two women hugged and interacted assured him that they were close.

Amanda was the complete opposite or Robin in appearance with her punk fifties style outfit of black leggings, a red-and-white checkered blouse, red heels, her bright red lipstick, and classic makeup. To top the look off, her raven hair was up in a bun on top of her head and tied with a large red bow.

He instantly liked her when she walked over to him and gave him a big hug and whispered, "Thank you for taking care of my girl."

Amanda stood next to him while everyone worked around them, chatting easily about how she and Robin had met at a function shortly after Robin had arrived in California.

Three o'clock came around, but shooting hadn't even started. Robin and the other actors and actresses stood around in full costume, waiting as Marcus and a small team of people moved, arranged, or changed things in the background. They had even removed a few paintings from the walls, which were immediately packaged up by the château's staff and put away in a secure room. Some of the paintings were priceless, while others were copies. He had no idea which was which. Nor, he doubted, did anyone else at this point.

Before he snuck up to his rooms to log in to his meeting, he found Robin running over her lines with Tom Levi, whom he'd been introduced to earlier that morning.

"Meeting time?" Robin had asked him. He'd nodded and kissed her.

"I'll be back when I can," he promised, then he headed upstairs.

His meeting ran long and, after a very intense debate, ended on a positive note. Thankfully.

When he made his way back downstairs, there was a

large table of sandwiches set up just outside the main hall. He grabbed one and a soda and found everyone in the ballroom. When someone called, "Action," he stood back and watched Robin rush into the room, her long dress flowing behind her. A look of concern flooded her eyes as if she was late for something.

His first instinct was to rush to her. To help her. Then he watched as she ran directly into Tom and listened as their characters, Meg and Roger, interacted for the first time.

He had to admit, after a few takes, he got completely lost in the art of seeing each little detail Marcus pointed out. Robin's face was turned away from the camera too much. Tom's tone was too low. There was a boom microphone in the shot.

Each time they stopped and restarted, Blake got better at spotting what was wrong.

Finally, after more than two dozen takes, Marcus was content, and they moved on to the next scene.

The process continued until shortly before dark. Just as the sun was setting, they moved out onto the balcony. This scene, due to time constraints with the sunset, was shot in fewer than five tries.

"We'll have to get the rest tomorrow night," Marcus called out. "For now, let's move to the main staircase."

The entire entourage was moved into the main entrance. This time, however, there wasn't enough room for extras to stand around watching the process. Only a handful of people were allowed to stand behind the cameras and watch. Thankfully, he was one of those few.

Then he saw her standing at the top of his stairs, and he quite literally lost his breath.

CHAPTER THIRTEEN

She stood at the top of the stairs, mentally preparing herself, running her lines through her head. When her eyes caught Blake's eyes, everything, including her lines, fled from her mind.

The way he was looking at her had her heart stopping. Her vision narrowed until it was only the two of them in the crowded space. For the past few hours, she'd done everything she could to keep her focus. Every fiber of her knew that he was in the room. Every breath she took, she could smell his musky scent in the air.

The mask that she'd carefully built to turn herself into Meg was completely gone. Simply because he was looking at her the way he was.

When action was called, she fumbled her lines. Once, she even tripped on a step. Thankfully, Marcus called for a five-minute break after the third time she forgot a line.

"Are you doing okay?" Marcus asked her.

"Yeah." Her eyes returned to Blake's. "Just... need a moment," she said, walking past Marcus.

"Everything okay?" Blake asked her as she approached him.

Without stopping, she walked up and kissed him. Letting all her feelings pour from her lips to his.

She didn't register the claps or laughter at first. Then Blake chuckled and pulled back.

"I think we've given everyone a show." He rested his forehead to hers.

"I couldn't concentrate. Not with the way you were looking at me. I could feel your gaze burning through me." She smiled up at him.

His smile deepened. "Want me to leave?"

She shook her head and closed her eyes. "No, I think after that kiss I can finally concentrate."

He smiled. "Glad I could be of service." She smiled and, this time, when she stood at the top of the stairs, she shed everything that was Robin Stein and became Megan Turner, a twenty-one-year-old college student on a once-in-a-lifetime vacation who meets the man of her dreams, a suave millionaire recluse who doesn't trust anyone but falls for Meg's innocence.

The shooting ended shortly after one in the morning. When she and Blake finally climbed into bed, she dropped off like a rock. She woke shortly after sunrise when Blake snuck out of the bed.

She knew he had another meeting that morning and could hear him in the next room, talking in low tones. Rolling over, she pulled out her phone and, for the first time in a few days, scanned social media.

She held in a gasp when she ran across an article link with an image of her and Blake gazing into each other's eyes in front of the Eiffel Tower. She remembered being followed by the paparazzi and knew that the image was out there. What she hadn't expected was that the image would have turned out so…. perfect.

Smiling, she scanned through the misinformation and lies in the article until she found the photographer's name. She shot a message to Amanda, whom she knew was probably already awake in a room on the west wing.

"Morning. Can you look into purchasing this? Do we have to purchase it to save it?" She sent the text and a snapshot of the image.

Amanda's reply came back quickly. "On it. Will let you know. It's an amazing pic. For personal use or professional?"

"Personal," Robin replied.

"On it," Amanda replied.

Robin lay in bed, scanning a few more articles about her and Blake and the shooting. There were grainy photos of them that night, Blake's arm wrapped up.

She laughed at some of the crazy things they said. That Blake had been shot by Robin's ex, Joe Cline, a man she'd gone out on two dates with. Or that he'd been shot by Tom Levi, who was jealous since they'd fallen in love while filming *It Takes Two*.

There was absolutely nothing between her and Tom, outside of shooting. Actually, from the vibes she was getting from the man, she was pretty sure she wasn't on the right team to gain his attention.

"Quick answer. If it's on social media, you can save the image for personal pleasure," Amanda's answer came back.

Smiling, she found the photographer's social media links and saved the image. She thought about saying something to the woman, a thank-you of sorts, but instead sent a message to Amanda.

"Send something nice to the photographer as a thank

you. I think it's the best shot of me I've seen from the paparazzi."

Amanda sent back an emoji of a laughing face. "Will do." Then another message. "May I say... this place is amazeballs."

"I know," she replied. "Have you seen the library?"

"No! There's a library?" Amanda asked. "Girl, where?"

"I'll show you. Meet for breakfast in..." She glanced down at her phone and finished typing. "Half an hour?"

"Where?" Amanda asked. "I might get lost."

"Main Hall."

"I can find it. It's in the center of everything if I remember correctly. See you there," Amanda replied.

Robin jumped out of bed. She cleaned up and dressed in a pair of yoga pants and a T-shirt. Filming wasn't set to start until later that day.

Stepping out of the bedroom, she noticed Blake was done with his meeting and working on his computer.

"Morning." She walked over and kissed him.

"Morning." He smiled up at her.

"Done with your meetings?" she asked.

"One. I have another in ten minutes." He glanced at his watch. "Then another after that."

"I'm going to meet Amanda for breakfast. Need anything?" She straightened his tie. She loved seeing him dressed up, even if it was just the top half of him, as he wore a pair of sweats instead of dress pants. The first time she'd seen him like that, she'd laughed, but then realized it was pretty smart, considering all he had were virtual meetings. She found it sexy for some weird reason.

"Sounds fun. No, I'm set." He motioned to his coffee. "I had some toast and eggs delivered earlier since I'm stuck here for a while." He pulled her down and kissed her. "I'll find you later when I'm done here."

She lingered over the kiss before turning and heading out to find Amanda.

Having her friend there somehow made things more real. She showed Amanda the library and a few of her other favorite rooms before heading to the main dining room. There was a huge buffet set up along the wall and more than a dozen people were already enjoying the meal.

Since it was sunny out, she and Amanda took their plates outside and sat in the sunshine. They looked out over the rose garden while they ate and chatted.

"So, you and Blake seem serious," Amanda said when there was a break in the conversation.

"I've never felt so much for someone so quickly," she admitted. "It's kind of scary how not scared I am. Is that weird?"

Amanda laughed. "Girl, when it's right, time stands still."

Robin relaxed back and glanced out over the perfectly manicured lawn and flowers.

"I wasn't looking to get into a relationship," she said.

"That's when it usually comes out of left field and bam." Amanda clapped her hands together. "Hits you from the side and knocks you on your ass."

Robin smiled. "Is that what happened with you and Stan?"

"Stan's just my sex toy," Amanda said with a smirk, causing Robin to laugh.

"Right. Does he know that?" Robin asked.

"Oh, we have an agreement." Amanda winked.

Just then, several more of the crew came out and joined them on the patio, and conversation turned towards filming.

She had worked with the crew over the past few months. There were a few new faces, but for the most part, she knew everyone.

It didn't surprise her to have Javan following her around. She was used to having a security detail while she was in the States.

But this morning, it was Blake's brother-in-law following her around instead. Ethan Knight was a legend, or at least Blake described him as such. The man was an impressive piece of meat. His shoulders were easily twice as wide as Blake's. But all those muscles weren't her type. Impressive, yes, but she much preferred a lean, toned runner's body.

Ethan was married to Ann, Blake's sister. Ann was a national treasure in the newscasting business. Currently, the station she worked for was number one in the nation. She had reached primetime status shortly after her big exposé about her father's assistant, Paul, and his attempt to assassinate her father. Of course, the story of how Ann and Ethan had escaped Brazil was an even bigger legend. Many people had tried to turn the tale into a movie shortly after the incident had taken place. To date, the only version was a half-cocked tale of what Robin assumed were half-truths. There was no way anyone would survive a fall off a cliff.

Thinking about that, she figured that the next chance she'd get, she'd ask Ethan about it personally.

"You disappeared," Amanda said, breaking into her thoughts.

She shook her head clear and smiled. "Sorry." Her eyes moved to Ethan. The man was watching her and yet his eyes scanned the growing crowd on the balcony at the same time.

"Blake's brother-in-law is impressive and scary at the same time," Amanda said under her breath.

"Yeah." She leaned forward and lowered her voice. "I was just thinking of the story of what happened to him and Blake's sister in Brazil. Do you think all of that happened?"

Amanda's eyes moved to Ethan. "He was shot saving the senator. Senior, that is."

"Yeah." Both of them glanced at Ethan again. Then Amanda shocked her by waving the man over towards them. She kicked her friend under the table as Ethan moved over to them.

"We didn't get introduced yesterday. I'm Amanda Hughes, Robin's fragent." She smiled. "That's friend and agent." It was a standing joke between them since the two of them had more than just a professional relationship.

Ethan shook Amanda's hand. "Ethan Knight."

"Join us?" Amanda motioned to the empty chair. Ethan sat down and instantly looked less intimidating. "So." She leaned closer to Ethan. "Are all the stories we've heard about you true?"

Ethan chuckled. "Depends. What have you heard?" His eyes moved to hers as Amanda nudged her under the table. Talk about putting her on the spot.

"Oh, okay, my turn, I guess," she said with a chuckle. "Did you and Ann slide down and fall off a cliff in a Brazilian jungle?"

His smile widened. "Yup."

She thought about it. "Seriously?"

"Yup." He relaxed back slightly. "We were escaping the ring of kidnappers hunting Ann and ran head-on into a drug cartel who didn't like us knowing what they were up to. It had rained the night before and as we were escaping..." He shrugged. "Slid down a muddy hill. Then, to escape, we went off a cliff into the rapids." He frowned slightly. "I don't recommend it."

"I bet not," Amanda said. "What about the bit about the two of you stowing away in a crate?"

"Yup, most of what was in that cheesy flick is true. Not sure how they got some of it." He frowned again.

"What about the part about the hotel in Brazil exploding? Did you carry Ann out of a burning building?" Amanda asked.

Ethan nodded his head and both women looked at him in awe.

"The only part that wasn't true was the bit about me fighting off a dozen bad guys single-handedly at the senator's event at the University of Texas," Ethan added. "There were only two of them."

"It's another reason I call him GI Joe," Blake said with a chuckle from behind them. He walked forward and slapped Ethan on the shoulder and then set a cup of coffee down in front of the man. "Thought you could use a pick-me-up."

"Thanks, bro," Ethan said easily as Blake took the seat next to Robin.

"Morning," Blake said to Amanda. "Sleep well?"

"Like a stone." Amanda smiled. "You have an amazing place here. The library." She held her hands over her heart. "If I wasn't happily married, I'd marry you just for that room alone."

Blake laughed. "Spend as much time in there as you want."

"Oh, I plan on it," Amanda said. She glanced down at her watch when it chimed. "I'm going to run and check on a few things. See you later." She gathered her things and left.

"I like your fragent," Ethan said to her. "I don't like a lot of people from Hollywood." His eyes narrowed at her. "You're on that list too."

She smiled. "Thanks. You're not so bad for a GI Joe."

Ethan chuckled. "So, everything seems to be running smoothly."

"It is now. Thanks to you and Javan," she said easily. "Not that Blake didn't handle things amazingly."

"You're the one who saved my butt in Paris," Blake jumped in to remind her.

"You're the one who was shielding me from the bullets." She shivered as she thought about it. Then she reached up and ran her fingers over the cut on his arm, which had turned into a line across his perfect skin.

"Sounds like the two of you took care of each other," Ethan said. "Javan is running backgrounds on everyone." He motioned around them. "As well as looking into the threats Amanda has turned over to the other agency."

Robin dropped her hand and turned to Ethan. "Threats?" She frowned. Blake reached for her hand under the table. "What threats?"

Ethan glanced towards Blake. "I... I'm going to make my rounds." He quickly stood up and disappeared.

"What threats?" She turned towards Blake as her vision grayed. Had everyone been keeping something from her

She didn't know what hurt more, the fact that the people closest to her had hidden the danger from her or that she was just finding out that both Blake and Ethan knew before she did? And that Blake had kept it from her until now. Her heart hurt at the deception.

CHAPTER FOURTEEN

Blake could see the pain in Robin's eyes. Glancing around the balcony, he took her hand and pulled her up, and started walking towards the garden where they could talk in private.

When they stepped onto the cobblestone pathway, he turned down the pathway that led to the edge of the lake. A crisp white gazebo sat at the edge of the water.

He leaned against the railing and pulled her into his arms.

"Marcus mentioned that Amanda had been shielding you from a few..."—he took a deep breath— "credible threats towards you in the past year. Ethan contacted her and the PI she had looking into them. I was going to tell you. I just found out the other night."

She was tense in his arms but didn't pull away. He took that as a good sign.

"I didn't mean to keep it from you," he said into her hair and felt her immediately relax.

"I know, it's just... Amanda did. From the sounds of it, for almost a year." Robin sighed.

"No doubt she did it out of concern for you. Besides, she told Marcus that it's what you pay her for. To worry for you." He felt her relax even more.

"I'm sure you're right." She glanced up at him. "You'd want to know, right? If someone was threatening you?"

He nodded slowly. "Still, I don't pay someone to do that for me." He smiled.

"Other than Ethan and Javan?" she asked.

He rolled his eyes. "Okay, yeah, besides them. But we made an agreement about it long ago. Something tells me you and Amanda haven't discussed what to do in cases like this."

"You're right." She gasped. "Is that why I've had to change my phone number twice in the past few months?" He felt bad and nodded. "Marcus knew too?" she asked.

"He only knew because Amanda requested that he have more security while on-site," he explained.

She dropped her arms and took a few steps away from him. She leaned on the railing to overlook the water. A bunch of ducks happily floated on the calm surface. At one point in his childhood, there had been a pair of swans. But they had chased a few guests when they'd taken one of the rowboats out and so they'd had to be rehomed to a lake down the road.

Still, the ducks were peaceful enough to watch and a pleasure to feed occasionally.

"Are you okay?" he asked Robin, not wanting to crowd her.

She turned to him suddenly and smiled. "I will be. For now, I'm going to head in for hair and makeup." She started to walk away, then walked over to him and kissed him. "Thank you. For being honest with me."

"Any time."

"Do you think that it was the person... the same one who shot at us, that's been leaving me threats?" she asked. He could see the worry in her eyes, but he was not going to lie to her now.

"That's what we're all thinking."

He watched her process that information for a moment before shaking her head. "I... can't think about this right now." She crossed her arms over her chest as if she was cold in the warm sunlight. "I need to head back and prepare for today." He stood up straight, but she held up her hand to his chest. "I'd like some time alone." She lifted to her toes and kissed him again on the lips. His hands dropped to his side from her hips as she moved away.

She stopped just outside of the gazebo. "I'll see you inside?"

He nodded, not trusting his voice. Then he stood like a statue and watched her slowly make her way back to the château.

What was he doing? He should have told her what he knew the moment he'd found out. Turning back around towards the lake, he mentally berated himself for a few moments before heading back inside.

He knew for the next hour she would be locked in wardrobe, hair, and makeup, so he went and found Ethan. He desperately needed someone to talk to.

He found the man in the kitchen, appearing to flirt with the head chef, Alice, who was easily eighty years old.

"I'm telling Ann," he teased as he walked over and took a cookie from the plate Alice had been offering Ethan.

"Go ahead. Your sister knows my love for any woman who can cook like Alice," Ethan added with a wink.

"Taking a break?" he asked between bites.

"Javan is on shift. He likes watching them transform your woman with hair and makeup." When Alice moved away to get back to work, Ethan's voice dropped. "Looks like the two of you had a lot to talk about."

Blake sighed and nodded as he finished the cookie. "She was pretty upset I didn't tell her... what I had found out."

"Yeah." Ethan smiled. "I gathered that. Remember that first summer when we received more threats and you locked yourself in your room for an entire week? Don't think I didn't know it wasn't because you were afraid. You were pissed we were dancing around the idea of telling you. Then you overheard us and..." Ethan smiled. "You were one stubborn kid."

"Were?" Blake's eyebrows arched as he smiled.

Ethan laughed and slapped him on the back. "There's enough love in Robin's eyes when she looks at you I'm sure she is going to forgive you for this." He slapped him again on the shoulder and started walking out of the kitchen.

Love? Did Robin love him?

He knew his feelings for her. Hell, the moment he'd seen her, he'd fallen fast and hard. He'd been hoping that she'd felt the same for him. If his brother-in-law could see it, maybe Blake was just blind?

For the rest of the day, he watched them film the same scenes they had filmed the night before with several key changes. The lighting and camera angles were all different.

He always wondered how movies filmed the same scenes from different angles. Now he knew.

It was amazing. Robin and the rest of the actors recreated the same scenes over and over again, saying the same lines with the same pitch in their voices. The same small movements down to the way they held their hands.

It was as impressive to watch the actors as it was to watch the dance that happened behind the cameras. Everyone took a break for food shortly after five that evening, then continued filming outside as the sunset was in the background. Once again, the same scenes were filmed from different angles.

Finally, just before midnight, filming came to an end.

"Tomorrow we start the dream sequence," Marcus called out. "Shooting starts at eleven."

There were a few groans from the group before everyone dispersed.

"How are you feeling?" he asked Robin when she walked over to him and wrapped her arms around his waist.

"Tired," she said with a slight sigh. "Hungry." She smiled up at him. "What are the chances we can get something to eat and lie in bed watching a movie?"

He smiled. "I'd say chances are pretty good." He took her hand and led her back to the wardrobe room, where he knew her outfit would be hung up until it was needed again. Her makeup would be carefully removed by her, later, in their bathroom. Her long hair, which was carefully pinned up in an intricate braid and bun, would be let loose and tied in a looser braid for the night.

He waited outside the room while she changed into her clothes. Five minutes later, she walked out in the same yoga pants and shirt she'd been wearing earlier.

They were just heading down the hallway when Amanda came rushing towards Robin. He felt Robin tense slightly.

"Do you have a sec?" Amanda asked a little breathless.

Robin glanced at him and, seeing the look in her eyes, he dropped her hand and said, "I'll grab some food and meet you upstairs?" Robin nodded and turned to Amanda as he headed towards the kitchen.

He helped Esme, one of the kitchen staff, make a couple of ham sandwiches and heat some leftover soup. He added some chips and two apple turnovers to the tray and carried everything up the back staircase to their rooms.

Since Robin wasn't there yet, he changed into some sweats and logged in to deal with a few emails.

One email caught his eye immediately. The subject line said, "Urgent – your life is in my hands." He opened it and braced for what he knew was coming. He'd been expecting something ever since the shooting in Paris.

What he hadn't expected was the attached private photos of him and Robin on the grounds of the château earlier that day.

"Son of a..." He pulled out his cell phone and called Ethan.

"Yo?" Ethan answered on the second ring.

"I got an email. Got a moment?" he asked.

"I'm heading over. Javan's on shift." He could hear Ethan walking quickly. "Robin is still downstairs talking with Amanda."

"Yeah." He sighed. "I figured that."

There was a quick knock on the door and then Ethan stepped in.

Blake hadn't even read the message yet. With Ethan glancing over his shoulder, they read it together.

"ALL CONTACT WITH ROBIN STEIN WILL STOP IMMEDIATELY!" The first line was typed in all capital letters. "This is not negotiable. You have plenty of secrets to unveil. The attached photos are proof that even you are not untouchable. The attached document is more proof that everything you do can be exposed."

Blake frowned as he glanced through the PDF that was attached.

"What is it?" Ethan asked.

"Just one of the bills I signed this morning." He shrugged slightly. "The document went out to more than a dozen people, any of which could have leaked it." He went back to the email and continued reading.

"You are to remove yourself from Château de Ferrières by midnight tomorrow night or you forfeit your life. I won't miss next time."

"No doubt it's from a bogus email address," Ethan said over his shoulder. "What about the images? Can you tell where they were taken from?"

He opened the images again. "Across the lake." He thought back to when he and Robin had been standing there earlier that morning, trying to remember if he'd seen anyone across the water. The truth was, he'd been too into their conversation to pay any attention.

"That's still your property, right?" Ethan asked.

"Yes and no. Most of it is, but there's a patch that belongs to the nearest neighbors. This could be from that patch."

"For now, there is no proof that this person has access to the château. But they could want us to believe that. At least we know why you were shot at now," Ethan added.

Just then the door opened, and Robin came in. Seeing Ethan and Blake at the computer with the image of them at the gazebo, her smile fell away.

"What's that?" she asked.

Ethan straightened up. "Forward me a copy," he said before disappearing.

Blake hit forward and send then turned towards Robin, who had moved closer.

"I just got this." He motioned to the screen and stood up, giving her the chair. He stood silently, letting the words and images sink in.

"It is about me," she said softly as she turned. "What is Ethan going to do about it?"

"Now?" He shrugged. "Probably frisk every single person on the grounds before putting a twenty-four-seven detail on us both." He pulled Robin up and wrapped his arms around her.

"You... aren't going to leave?" she asked into his chest.

"No, I wouldn't leave you here alone. Exposed."

"But—"

He looked into her eyes and cupped her face.

"They threatened me. Not you. That doesn't mean they don't want to harm you," he said, feeling his gut twist.

"I don't want you hurt because of me again," she said softly as tears pooled in her eyes.

"They won't be given the chance to touch me," he said. "How about we sit down, have some food, and watch a movie?"

Robin sighed and rested her head against his chest. "I'm too tired to think right now." She leaned into him.

"How did things go with Amanda?" He instantly felt her tense again.

"I get why she did what she did. But I don't condone it." She sighed heavily and glanced up at him again. "But I can forgive her. She's promised to keep me in the loop." She glanced down at the computer screen. "Which means you should probably forward a copy of that to her as well."

He dropped his hold on her and leaned over. "What's her email address?" After sending a copy off to Amanda, they went into the bedroom. Robin changed into those sexy pink shorts and tank top, and they settled down to eat in bed and watch a movie.

Amanda called less than ten minutes later, and he sat by and listened as Robin explained that Ethan was looking into it and that Blake was safer here than anywhere else. Just hearing her say those words made him relax. After all, it was true. He'd never been anywhere else in the world that he'd felt as safe. Especially if Robin was safe and by his side.

CHAPTER FIFTEEN

Robin had a difficult time sleeping that night. The next morning, she tried not to let her worry show, but when she sat down for hair and makeup, she kept glancing over nervously at Blake, whom she'd demanded not leave her side all day. Javan sat in the corner of the room, looking entertained as Carlos and Carmen turned her into the fantasy Meg for the dream sequence.

The white eighteenth-century period dress, complete with a massive hoop skirt, had to be put on before the finishing touches so as not to damage the intricate Victorian braid and buns, which had been beefed up with hair extensions.

She sat in the chair in the massive dress, watching her reflection turn into that of a fairytale princess.

"Wow," Blake said from his chair. "Just... wow. Is that what every woman had to go through back then?"

"Back then?" Carmen asked with a chuckle. "You do see what we put Robin through every day?"

Blake smiled. "Normally you don't have to tie her into a dress like that."

"I'm thankful corsets went out of fashion long ago," Robin said, standing up and twirling the massive skirt while she checked her reflection in the standing mirrors. "Still, it does make my waist tiny."

"It was tiny to begin with," Blake said, making her smile.

"Thank you." She walked towards him and when her skirts bumped into his legs, she laughed. "How did people kiss back then?" she asked.

"They didn't," Carmen and Carlos said at the same time, then both of them burst out laughing.

"Which is why in the dream sequence, you're dancing with yourself," Carmen said with a smile. "All eyes will be on you anyway."

"I know I can't take mine off you," Blake said, making her heart do little jumps in her chest.

"No more of that," Carmen said, nudging Robin forward. "Any more blushing and I'm going to have to redo your makeup."

Robin was smiling as she made her way out to the ballroom, where part of the dream sequence would be filmed.

When she noticed Ethan enter the room almost an hour after filming had started, she wanted to ask him if he had any updates.

This scene had a very intricate dance sequence, which she had been trained for weeks earlier. Now, however, in the massive skirt, the choreographer had to adjust a few moves. That ate up some of the time while everyone stood around waiting and watching.

Finally, when action was called, she glided into the ballroom. All the decorations had been replaced with all-white, sequin-covered items. She knew that whatever hadn't been replaced would be easily changed in postproduction.

For the next two hours, she danced in the ballroom. When Marcus was happy with all the shots and angles, they moved out to the main stairwell.

An hour later, she was breathless, and her legs were burning from running up twenty steps more than two dozen times while trying to make it look effortless.

"We'll take a short break," Marcus called out to the room. "We'll film the outside balcony shots at sunset. For now, you can change and rest. Grab something to eat," he said.

"Need to change?" he asked her, nodding towards the massive dress.

"Yes, please." She sighed and started walking down the hallway towards the room that had been designated as the dressing rooms.

He stood outside while she changed once more into a pair of yoga pants and a T-shirt. Her hair and makeup would be touched up later after she donned the dress again.

They made their way to the dining hall along with everyone else. This time, however, they sat inside and ate.

They'd been given strict orders from Ethan to stay inside as much as possible, something she was going to make sure Blake did. She wasn't going to chance Blake's life. Just thinking of those images of them standing on the bank of the lake made her shiver.

"Cold?" Blake asked her.

"No," she replied, but she leaned into his side a little more. "Just tired. With as many times as I ran up those stairs, I think I can skip the gym this week," she joked.

"Well, no one would ever know. You looked amazing and it looked effortless." He wrapped his arm around her.

"Thanks. We have another hour before I need to head to wardrobe again. I'd like to find someplace quiet to shut down." She thought about heading back up to their rooms and napping. But she'd probably wake up more tired than if she'd just sat somewhere quiet with him.

"We can head to the library?" he suggested.

"Perfect." It was wonderful how Blake seemed to be able to read her thoughts. It was as if they'd known each other longer than just a week.

Had it only been a week? How had it been only one week?

As they made their way towards the library, he talked about her work. About how exciting it was to see the filming process.

She'd been in the industry for a few years now, but hearing his excitement about what she considered to be mundane, she grew excited herself.

When they stepped into the library, she was smiling and laughing. Until she noticed Amanda crying on the sofa.

"What's happened?" she asked, rushing towards her friend.

"It's... nothing." Amanda wiped her eyes.

Robin glanced over Amanda's head at Blake, who motioned towards the door. "I'll... get us some tea and cakes."

"Hey." Robin wrapped her arms around Amanda. "What is it? Is Stan okay?"

"Yes, it's just... I lost a client," Amanda said with a sigh. "I hate when that happens." She rolled her eyes.

"Oh no. Who?" Robin asked. Of course Amanda had other clients. Hell, at this point, she was responsible for more than four A-listers in Hollywood.

"Rachael Osborne," Amanda said with a sniffle. "Rachael said she didn't like the way I'd handled her last contract. She accused me of playing favorites with you." Amanda smiled at her through her tears.

"You do play favorites." Robin hugged her. "Because I'm the best." The joke did what she'd intended it to. Hearing Amanda's laughter warmed her heart. "Rachael doesn't know what she's letting go of," she added. "She's never going to make it in Hollywood without you."

Amanda smiled even more. "Thanks, I needed to hear that. Even if it's not true."

"What are friends for?" She hugged Amanda again just as Blake stepped in holding a tray of tea and more of the tiny cakes she enjoyed.

"What are those?" Amanda asked, motioning to the cakes.

"Sin," Blake answered with a smile. "Feeling better?"

"I will be after I have about a dozen of those," Amanda said, taking a chocolate cake and plopping it in her mouth. "Maybe two dozen."

For more than half an hour, the three of them sat in the library, laughing and enjoying the cakes and tea. When it was time for Robin to head back to get ready for the evening filming, they all walked down together.

Filming resumed, and the closer it grew to midnight, the more anxious she grew. Blake, for his part, looked relaxed and quite at home. She mentally laughed, considering this was his home.

She wondered what she would do if she'd been threatened and told to leave her own apartment. There was no doubt that she'd leave it and the entire city if she had to. Hell, at this point, there wasn't anything in the apartment that she couldn't live without. Anything that she held dear, she always took with her. The small picture book Claire had given her when she'd left for California long ago. The matching bracelets she'd bought the last time Claire had come out to visit her. Everything else that she valued was digital. All the memories she'd uploaded each time she'd visited her dad or places she'd wanted to travel.

When they took another break so that her hair could be touched up, she glanced over at Blake and smiled at the thought of the image of them in front of the Eiffel Tower. That picture was now among the few things in life she treasured.

"How are you holding up?" Carlos asked her as he finished up.

"Looking forward to shooting this next scene." She smiled. "I've waited all year for it."

"I bet," Carmen added. "It's the reverse Cinderella scene."

Robin laughed. "Totally. I mean, seeing your prince at the base of the stairs for a moment before he rushes off and you can't find out who he is for the rest of the party and then drifting into a dream sequence that rivals every fairy-tale." She sighed as she smiled at Blake.

"I thought your characters met for the first time inside the ballroom?" Blake asked.

"We see each other for the first time outside, then Tom's character, Roger, is pulled away for an important meeting, which consumes the rest of the party. Just when Meg starts to think she'd imagined her dream man, she bumps into him in the ballroom. The scenes we filmed yesterday," she answered. "The dream sequence starts out here when they first see one another, then moves into the ballroom, and ends when she starts to doubt herself."

"Makes sense." Blake shrugged. "There is so much I've learned about the process so far. It's all so very interesting."

She thought about his work and how much he'd put

aside to be there with her. Yet in all this time they'd been together, she hadn't even tried to learn more about his work.

Everyone knew what a senator's job entailed, right? They were voted into office, helped pass legislation, and were servants to the public. She understood there was probably a whole lot more to the job. After all, he was in Paris for meetings.

She'd heard about the summit but hadn't known what the main purpose was.

When they resumed shooting, she tried to focus on her work, to block out her own selfishness, and get her job done. After all, this scene was why she'd accepted the role.

After the first dozen or so cuts, Marcus pulled her aside while everyone reset for the shot.

"What's up?" Marcus asked her.

She knew better than to deny anything. She crossed her arms around herself and sighed.

"I've been extremely selfish," she said softly, her eyes moving over to where Blake sat chatting with Ethan.

"When it comes to love, we all deserve to be selfish occasionally," Marcus replied.

"No, I mean... He's given up his meetings to be here with me. He's opened his home." She motioned around. "He's putting his life on the line," she added with a whisper.

Marcus sighed. "And he's as lost in you as you are in him. There's a reason Ramon and I kept our relationship secret for so many years. Selfishness. Once it was out there, not only did my ex-wife get most of my shit, but it was no longer just us. I would give anything for my husband, but part of me wishes I could go back to before. To when we could be selfish. Lock ourselves away in a..." He glanced around and smiled slightly. "In a castle and ignore the world. Yes,..."—he waved his hand at her— "I know we're all here watching the show. But for two days, it was just the two of you. I think your man knows that once things get to some sort of normal, you are more than all this."

She sighed and glanced over to where Blake was watching her. The smile on his lips and the look in his eyes ensured her that he felt just as strongly towards her as she did about him.

"You're right." She smiled at Marcus. "How'd you get to be so smart?"

Marcus laughed. "Practice." He touched her shoulder. "Ready to get back at it?"

She nodded and, this time, she nailed the scene.

CHAPTER SIXTEEN

One more day of filming. That's all they had left. Blake wanted to hold onto this time at the château for as long as he could. He enjoyed having the place filled with people he knew and liked. Plus, he enjoyed spending this magical time with Robin.

Midnight had come and gone, and Ethan and his team, which included five of his best security details, were now keeping watch twenty-four seven. He knew once they returned to the States in two days, Javan and Ethan would be there for his safety.

Still, he didn't want real life to get in the way of his and Robin's perfect fantasy life there at the château.

His meetings were growing longer each day he stayed away from his work. His two PAs were making excuses with the press, who were demanding a statement about the shooting. It was all anyone could talk about back in the States.

"The two of you are this year's 'It' couple," Leslie told him over the video conference. Jeffery rolled his eyes.

"It's disgusting that you're more popular because of who

you are dating, but it's true. Forget all the hard work you did to get clean drinking water to your state or the changes you put in place for schools to educate more kids." Jeffery sighed. "All anyone can talk about is who you're shacking up with."

Blake chuckled since he knew the drill. Still, as long as the publicity was good, and kept Robin safe, there was little he could do to stop it.

"For now, as long as it's all good, we'll be okay." He thought about the new threats he'd received in his email. All of them were most likely from the same person, even though they were all from different email addresses. There wasn't anything new, just a bunch of the same stuff. Leave or I won't miss next time.

Still, the fact that there weren't any more pictures attached confirmed that they didn't have access to the grounds. Ethan had hiked out to the other side of the lake shortly after the first email and had set up a trail camera to try and catch a glimpse of whoever was sending the messages or at least whoever had taken the photos.

So far, the camera had only caught sight of a few owls, some bunnies, a fox, and deer peacefully grazing. He hadn't known there was so much wildlife on the grounds. It made him want to preserve it even more.

Back home in Georgia, there was pretty much the same types of wildlife. He had set in place safeguards to preserve what he could. It was something his father was passionate about as well.

He loved his yearly hunting and camping trips with his father, which they'd started taking shortly after his kidnapping. If anything, he and his father had grown closer after that fateful day.

"You're quiet." Amanda broke into Blake's thoughts.

"Hm?" He glanced over to the chair next to him, where Robin's agent sat, balancing a laptop on her knees.

"Just watching the show." He motioned to the team of people working to change the dream ballroom back into the real ballroom for another shot.

"I know someone deep in thought when I see them." Amanda shut her laptop and shifted to look at him. "Second thoughts on all this?"

"Hell no," he answered quickly. "I'm loving this. It would be wonderful for this to stretch out. But since this place is booked in a few days..." He sighed. "We'll have to clear out."

Amanda smiled. "What about Robin going home with you?"

"Can't wait to show her around and for her to meet the fam," he said with a smile. "What about you? Heading back to the West Coast? Back to the spotlights."

Amanda chuckled. "Honey, I get to stand behind them, never in them. But, yeah, I miss my fam."

In the past few days, he'd grown to like Amanda. She was brutally honest and funny as hell. Not to mention a very loyal friend to Robin.

"Okay, so if all is well, why the frown?" she asked, crossing her legs. Today's outfit consisted of a red polka dot flare skirt, a black button-up shirt, and a matching polka dot scarf tying her long black hair back. She finished the assemble with some Dr. Martens.

"Just deep in thought." He didn't really want to go into his fears about what might happen if they ever let their guard down. What would they do if whoever was making the threats was never caught?

"Hey." Amanda laid a hand on his arm. "They're going

to catch this creep. Your brother-in-law hasn't stopped working since he got here."

"Yeah," he agreed quickly as Marcus called quiet on the set once more. Glancing at his watch, he saw he had less than fifteen minutes before he was due to be on another meeting call. When filming paused again, he slid out of the chair and made his way up to his room.

His hand was on the doorknob when he felt a shiver race through his spine. Glancing over his shoulder, he saw a shadow cross the end of the hallway near the hidden staircase.

Since only a handful of the staff knew about it, he brushed it off and turned the doorhandle. Without warning, he was thrown back against the opposite wall.

It felt as if the entire château shook. He heard glass break, wood snap, and for a moment, he was weightless, just before the wind was knocked out of him. Black smoke filled the corridor quickly as a loud ringing filled his ears. His head spun.

Reaching up, he brushed his hand against the back of his head, where the worst of his pain was. His fingers came away wet. He saw the dark red blood covering his hand, and then glanced up to see Ethan running towards him, screaming. Blake could only hear the ringing while Ethan's mouth moved and concern flooded his brother-in-law's eyes.

"Sorry, GI Joe," he said with a cough just as everything went dark.

***

Robin was mid-line when the large chandelier hanging over the front entrance staircase shook so hard, she thought it was going to come crashing down on top of the camera crew set up directly underneath it.

She didn't know if she screamed, but several other people's screams rang out through the room. When the shaking stopped, her first thought was of Blake.

Her eyes scanned the chair he'd been sitting in moments before, only to see Amanda standing there, her hands over her mouth as she looked in horror at the chandelier.

"What was that?" someone asked.

"Javan?" She glanced over to where the man was rushing towards her.

"We have to go." He took her arm and pulled her towards the doors.

"No, wait. Blake," she cried out, trying to break free.

"Now," Javan said more firmly.

Instead of dragging her out the main doorway, he pushed on a panel and pulled her into a small hallway.

"Where—?" she asked, glancing around. Blake hadn't shown her this hidden passage. Where did it go? Where was Blake? What was that noise?

"This will lead us to a safe room we've set up," Javan said, peering around a corner where the hallway split off. She could see light coming from one of the directions, but they turned towards the darkness instead. "Come on." He pulled her along. "Quicker."

They rushed down the narrow hallway, and she was thankful she wasn't in her dream dress, since she doubted the thing would have fit in the confined space.

They turned two more corners and finally came to a large metal door with a new code lock on the handle. Javan punched the numbers in and shoved her inside before stepping inside himself.

"The bird is secure," he said into a small walkie-talkie. He stopped and listened, his dark eyes going to hers. She noticed instantly when concern flooded them. "Understood." He sighed and walked over to a large wall of computer screens.

She followed him and watched as he flipped from scene after scene. More than four dozen different scenes filled the screens, and she thought there must be a camera down every corridor in the building.

Then an image of Ethan hovering over a dark mass on the floor filled the television screen, and she cried out.

"Blake." She rushed forward. "What..."

Smoke filled the entire hallway. There were chunks of walls, wood, and furniture everywhere around him. Since the image was black and white, she couldn't tell if he was bleeding. Only that he was unconscious.

She turned to leave, but Javan grabbed her wrist, stopping her.

"Nope, we stay put," Javan said firmly.

"I have to go to him," she cried out as tears blinded her vision.

"Here." Javan placed a hand softly on her shoulders. "Sit. I'll get you something to drink."

She sat down in the chair he nudged her into and stared at the screen as Ethan hunched over Blake's body, gun drawn. He applied pressure to Blake's shoulder and talked into his phone. Smoke continued to bellow out of what used to be their rooms.

"Here." Javan handed her bottled water and then moved to sit down at the computer again. He continued to flip through the images. It took her a moment to realize he was going back in time and watching what had happened before the fire.

She blinked so she could watch, needing to know herself.

They watched a male figure in a dark hoodie and pants and carrying a tray knock on their door. A moment later, as if he knew the room was empty, he opened it and stepped inside.

Javan forwarded the image until the door opened again.

"Eight minutes inside," he said to himself.

They watched as the figure rounded the corner seconds before Blake stepped into the hallway.

She wanted to cry out, to get him to stop, but she knew it was too late. Blake paused at the door, looking off to where the figure had just disappeared. Then he turned back towards the door. The next moment, the camera shook, and she cried out as she watched Blake be thrown across the hall. He hit the wall and crumpled to the ground as smoke blocked the screen momentarily.

Then Javan was changing the image again.

"Where'd he go?" Javan said to himself. Several images flashed on the set before the dark figure was spotted rushing from the servant's entrance on the lowest floor.

"The building is clear," Javan said into the walkie-talkie. "Medics are at the gate," he said, after flipping to another screen. He hit a button and she watched the gates slide open and the ambulance rush through.

How long had they been in that room? The passage of time was only marked by what she saw on the screens. When Javan flipped back to the hallway where Ethan and Blake were, she noticed Ethan had holstered his weapon and was now concentrating only on Blake. Two more of his men were there, standing over them, watching or helping.

She wanted—no, needed—to go to him.

She stood up again and reached the door before Javan could stop her this time.

"I'm going to him," she said in a firm voice.

Javan's dark eyes searched hers before he nodded. "Head to the right, the second corridor on the left. Take the stairs to the third floor, and turn left." He turned back to the computer screens.

"Thanks," she said and rushed from the room.

She ran down the dark hallway, playing over the instructions in her head as she went. She vaguely remembered being in this part of the château before, and when she came out of the hidden staircase by where their rooms had been, she realized just where she'd been.

Then she saw Blake lying there, unconscious, bleeding, and hurt, and nothing else mattered besides getting to him and making sure he was okay.

"Blake," she cried out as she knelt beside him.

"He's out," Ethan said, glancing around. "Where's Javan?"

"He let me come to him."

"You shouldn't..." Ethan started, but she glared at him. "Fine. Here, hold this." He motioned to the towel he was holding on Ethan's shoulder. With shaky hands, she put her hands over the towel to stop the bleeding on the massive tear in Blake's skin. This was nothing like the scratch he'd gotten from the glass in Paris. This was deep, and the blood was so dark.

"He's hit his head," Ethan said, gently moving around until he could see the back of Blake's head. "Yup, a huge knot here," he said in a low tone. When she noticed his hands come away covered in blood, she cried out. "No, you keep pressure there. I've got this. Head wounds always bleed more." He reached for another clean towel from one of his men standing over them.

For the next few minutes, they did their best to stop Blake's blood from leaving him. Then the paramedics arrived, and she stood back as the experts worked on him instead.

She rushed along with the gurney and even tried to help them maneuver it through the narrow halls and down the staircase.

When they reached the main floor, the entire crew stood back and watched them wheel Blake out. Marcus quickly handed her the jacket she'd worn earlier and her cell phone, which had been sitting on her chair while she'd filmed.

"Keep us posted," he said to her and kissed her cheek. "We'll be here."

She nodded and rushed to jump in the back of the ambulance. No matter what happened now, she wasn't going to be separated from Blake again. Wherever he went, she was determined to be there.

CHAPTER SEVENTEEN

The noise was killing his head, making it pulse. He tried to reach up and cover his ears, but his arms didn't work.

When he cracked open his eyes, he winced at the pain the bright lights caused.

"Easy," someone said softly with a very rich French accent.

His vision was too blurry to see who it was and, after a moment, he gave up trying to figure it out.

"I'm here," Robin's voice came suddenly.

"Robin?" He jerked and opened his eyes again, and the pain shot through him even more.

"Yes," she said with a sob. "I'm right here. Lay back. We've got you. They need you to lay still," she said suddenly. "They're trying to stitch you up."

He felt it now, the numbness and the slight tugging on his shoulder. "What happened?" he asked, trying to hold still.

She was quiet for a moment and only spoke when he opened his eyes.

"There was a bomb," Robin said softly.

He tried to remember, but everything was too fuzzy, and all he could concentrate on was the high-pitched buzzing in his head.

"Rest," Robin said softly. "I'm here. I won't leave your side. Ethan's here too."

"Hey, brother," Ethan's reply came from somewhere behind him. "How are you holding up?"

"Hanging in there," he said with a slight groan. "If someone would stop the world from spinning, I'd appreciate it."

He heard Ethan chuckle. "He's going to be okay."

"Says the man who didn't get blown up." He groaned. He'd meant it as a joke, but when he heard Robin sniffle, he searched around for her. "I'm sorry. Too soon."

"Someday, when we're old, we'll joke about this, but for now, allow me my tears," Robin said.

"We're finished here." The first voice was back. "Once we get the X-rays back, we'll move him to a private room."

He closed his eyes and rested back as the room grew quiet. He woke again when he felt himself being wheeled down the hallway.

"I'm still here." Robin's voice had him glancing over next to him. Now he could see an outline of a figure next to him. "We're just moving you to a private room."

"My parents?" he asked. He'd wanted to ask Ethan to call them earlier, but he'd fallen asleep before he was able to.

"Ethan called them. They and your sister are on their way," Robin answered.

He closed his eyes again when the lights and movement caused his head to ache too badly. He listened as they settled him into a private room and heard the medical team leave. When everything grew quiet, he felt Robin settle on the bed next to him.

"How are you feeling?" she asked.

"Tired," he answered after assessing himself. "Was anyone else hurt?"

"No, just you," Ethan answered. His voice assured Blake that he was across the room, no doubt lounging in a chair somewhere, prepared to stay until Javan or someone else from his team replaced him.

"The château?" he asked, feeling Robin's hand take his. He gave it a light squeeze and relaxed, knowing she'd been far away from the blast.

"Your rooms are charcoal. The rest is fine," Ethan answered. "We'll need some fresh paint in the hallway and new rugs, but other than that..."

"Did you catch the guy?" he asked.

The room grew quiet for a moment. "No," Robin answered. "But we caught him on camera."

"Who?" he asked, wanting not to talk too much.

"Don't know. We couldn't see his face. We have his height and weight and how he got inside and out. Through the laundry room door. He used the back stairs, not the hidden ones, to go up and down. Javan's checking with the staff and everyone else to see if anyone happened to see him. We're also checking the rest of the security footage," Ethan answered.

"Right," he sighed. "I'm going to rest."

"He didn't even ask how badly he was hurt," he heard Robin say as he drifted off.

In truth, he knew exactly how badly he was hurt. From the numbness in his shoulder, he guessed he'd gotten more than a dozen stitches. It had felt that way when they'd been tugging on his skin. He could feel a golf-sized bump on the back of his head. It had probably bled since there was a massive bandage running around his head.

Other than that, his left ankle hurt, his right elbow, and his ass where it had hit the wall. The rest was scratches and bruising, which he figured he could deal with later.

"Blake?" The soothing voice of his mother woke him from the hazy dream. He'd been holding Robin as they stood by the lake, watching a pair of golden swans swim peacefully in the water. Three little versions darted around the parents as they all cut through the perfectly still waters.

"Mom?" He groaned. Suddenly, his mind blurred and he was eight years old again. GI Joe had just rescued him from the bad men who had wanted to kill him. His little body ached so bad from where the men had beat him unconscious. "I hurt," he groaned.

"I know, baby. We're all here now," his mother replied. "Can he have something to ease the pain?"

"I will ask the doctor," a woman said in a thick French accent.

Blake's eyes flew open. He was in Paris. Not Georgia. It had been a bomb, not three mad men trying to extort his father for money.

"Mom?" He blinked a few times and his mother's jet-black hair came into view. His mother was only ten years older than Ann but in the past few years, her toned body had rounded slightly. Still, she was tan and in good enough shape that most men stopped and enjoyed a look when she passed them by.

On more than one occasion, his friends had mentioned how hot his mother was. He used to catch his mother flirting with men all the time, which also upset him. It stopped bothering him somewhere in high school when his mother confessed how much she loved his father.

Since he'd moved out, his parents had only grown closer together. It warmed his heart just knowing that. Ann's relationship with his mother had grown as well. When he'd been young, she'd been distant towards Coleen. But after his kidnapping, the women had seemed to grow closer. Or at least they'd tolerated one another better.

"I'm here too, shorty." Ann's voice had him turning slightly. The room spun, and he groaned a little.

"Don't move too much," Robin said from somewhere in the room.

He reached out his hand, eager to touch any of his family or Robin.

When his father's beefy hand took his, he sighed. "Dad?"

"Yup. I heard you made a mess in your rooms," his father said. He probably hadn't meant it as a joke, since the ex-senator was serious most of the time, but still, Blake heard a couple of chuckles in the room, including Ethan's.

"Everyone's here?" he asked.

"For now, until they kick us out. The kids are back at the hotel," Ann answered. "With Javan."

"Right." He sighed. "What time is it?" he asked, closing his eyes again.

"A quarter past eleven," his father answered after a moment.

"Morning or night?"

"Morning," his mother answered.

"What day?"

The room was quiet again. "The bombing was yesterday," Robin answered. "You needed the sleep. You were in and out, but they said the medicine would play havoc with your memories."

"Right." He sighed. "What's the news saying about this?"

"A damned lot," Ethan answered. "Too much."

"Any idea who yet?" he asked, not wanting to open his eyes.

"Nope," Ethan answered quickly.

Blake thought for a moment, letting his mind circle back, settle, function again. "Mom, Dad, Ann, this is Robin."

Several chuckles greeted him.

"We've met," his mother responded. "Had breakfast together. About to have lunch together too."

"I could eat." His stomach growled.

"That's a good sign," Ethan said, and he heard his brother-in-law get up, no doubt to hug Ann, who could be heard sniffling quietly.

"We're going to head out. Grab the kids and get some lunch. Corey's just outside," Ethan said. "We'll be back later."

"Ethan." He opened his eyes and could see his brother-in-law's and sister's outlines. "Thanks." Ethan nodded, and he watched them leave. Then he turned to his parents. "Bring me back a burger?"

His father laughed; his mother frowned. "I don't think you're allowed—"

"Coleen, come on. We'll see what we can do," his father said, taking his mother's hand and pulling her towards the door.

Then Blake turned to Robin, who was standing against the wall, watching him. She was wearing a pair of yoga pants and a sweatshirt, so at least she'd gotten some fresh clothes and wasn't still in the ball gown. Then he realized that all her things, as well as his, were probably gone.

"Sorry about your stuff," he said, holding out his hand for her to come closer.

She shrugged as she walked. "It's just stuff." She sat on the edge of the bed and took his hand. "You are the most important thing to me. I can replace the rest."

He reached up with his right arm and cursed when the tubes taped to his hand yanked, and the I.V. line almost pulled free. "I want to put my arm around you." He groaned.

"For now, this will have to do." She leaned in and rested next to his side. She laid her head on his good shoulder, acting as if she was afraid that he'd break. In all honesty, he felt like he would at the moment.

"When can we go home?" he asked, half asleep.

"They're talking about releasing you as soon as tomorrow. If you're up for it," Robin answered.

"Good. We can fly home with my family," he said. "What about filming?"

"Marcus has assured me that he got everything he needed. They've packed up already and have left the château. Marcus and a few of the crew stopped by." She motioned to a table full of flowers. "From them."

"I'll have to remember to thank them," he said before he fell asleep again.

He woke when his parents came back in with a burger from one of the American fast-food places down the street. While he ate, they talked about all the press outside the hospital.

His father turned on the news and turned the volume to low. The food was making all the small hurts feel better. The news wasn't.

The stories ranged from Blake throwing himself in front

of the bomb to save Robin to him being a complete idiot and exploding the château himself in an accident.

"They just can't get their shit together," his father said in a low tone. "Reminds me of when your sister and Ethan took down my old assistant, Paul."

"It took a press conference then to get all the details right. You may have to step out there and tell them what's what," his mother said to his dad.

His father glanced at him and sighed. "Just say the word, son, and I'll get back in front of the cameras."

"Thanks." He glanced over at Robin, who was looking at him with such love and worry in her eyes that it almost hurt. "But I'll do this one myself. They're going to release me tomorrow. You can call a conference as we leave here and head to the airport," he told his father.

His dad smiled and nodded. "I'll arrange it."

"They're going to let you leave so soon?" his mother asked, changing the conversation to his health.

CHAPTER EIGHTEEN

Robin didn't like talking in front of live cameras. Especially about something so personal. Still, she stood by Blake while he half-leaned on a table that held more than a dozen microphones. Camera flashes blinded them.

When he started talking, the flashes died down a little.

"Thank you all for coming on such short notice," he said, earning a few laughs. "First things first. I'm fine. No broken bones, except this one." He touched the bandage wrapped around his head and gently tapped his forehead, earning more laughs. "We wanted to squash a few very badly made-up rumors. First off, yes, Robin and I are seeing one another." He glanced at her, and she smiled. They'd talked about this. She hadn't been happy he was going to be putting himself out there again for whoever was trying to kill him. But he and Ethan insisted that it was for the best. So she smiled and gave his arm a slight squeeze as more pictures were taken. Blake turned back to the cameras. "Second, yes, I did get blown up." He held up his hand. "No, I didn't do it cooking burgers, as was reported." He gave the press a half-smile and glanced down at her. "It's true, twice on this trip a madman has tried to take me out because of this." He held up their joined hands. "I'm still here. And as Robin has agreed to come home with me to Georgia, it's looking like I'll be right here for a long while."

Robin's heart did a little skip as she tried desperately not to cry.

"If getting shot at and blown up has taught me anything, it's to hold onto what you love in your life." He squeezed her hand gently. "And you are something I love," he said to her.

Her knees would have buckled had he not had an arm around her. "I thought live television would be the perfect place to tell you," he whispered. Then he turned to the press. "That is either the dumbest thing I've ever done or the most romantic," he said to chuckles.

"Most romantic," Robin said quickly, gaining a bunch of oohing and aahing from the room.

Blake surprised her by leaning in and giving her a kiss that had her toes curling. "Later," he said softly, and she nodded in agreement.

"Now, for the rest," Blake said after clearing his throat.

For the rest of the press conference, Blake talked about the attack and all the threats both of them had been receiving. He talked about the filming and the movie and mentioned how honored he was that they had chosen the Château de Ferrières to film *It Takes Two*'s most romantic scenes. Then he mentioned again how he was heading back to the States and that they would be staying at his place in Georgia while he took some time off to recover.

As they rode in the private car towards the airport, she frowned down at her hands.

"I don't like this plan," she said to both Ethan and Blake.

"What?" Blake asked.

"You've put another target on your back." She turned towards him. They had talked about this, how exposing where they were going would just open the door to whoever was after him.

Blake and Ethan had come up with the plan. They had even contacted the FBI back in the States. Normally, when Blake was in DC, the United States Capitol Police were in charge of protecting him. However, since this was an official terrorist threat, the FBI and Homeland Security had gotten involved.

Blake took her hand now and squeezed it gently. "We can't keep looking over our shoulders. What happens when you go off to start filming another movie? Or just go to the grocery store without me? I can't and won't let you out of my sight until this maniac is dealt with."

She thought about Blake returning to his work. Alone. They couldn't always have Ethan and his team watching him. Not for the rest of their lives. She knew it was a solid plan. Knew that some of the best men and women in the States would be watching them as well. Protecting them. Still, it felt wrong. It felt... risky. Too risky.

Part of her wanted to run and hide. Go somewhere no one knew who they were. Stay locked up, isolated for as long as they could. But the rational part of her knew this was the only way.

She nodded and then looked out the car window until they reached the airport. Since most of her things had been in the room when the bomb had gone off, the only things she had in the small bag she carried through the airport were things Marcus had gathered up and saved out of the rubble. Thankfully, her laptop had been downstairs while she'd been filming, since she'd video conferenced her sister during a break. She had a couple of changes of clothes she'd left in the dressing room and the beloved sweater that she'd forgotten in the library the other night.

The rest of her things were gone and, as she'd told Blake, she was okay with it. It wasn't as if she couldn't replace her clothing and her toiletry items. Actually, she hardly ever traveled with most of it anyway since Carmen and Carlos were always on-site.

But heading to Georgia. That was personal.

"Mind if I dip in here for a moment?" she asked, motioning to a boutique shop in the main area of the airport. They were traveling in a large group that included Blake's family and Javan as they all headed to the plane together.

"I'll go with you," Ethan said and followed her inside.

While she looked around and found a couple of things she would purchase, including a blouse, a pair of jeans, and some toiletry items, Ethan stood behind her, his eyes on his family standing outside the glass windows waiting for her.

"Everything okay?" he asked her when she'd been staring at the same shirt for a few moments.

"Yes." She blinked and was mortified as a tear slipped down her cheek. "How do you do it?" she asked, wiping the tear away.

"What?" Ethan asked calmly.

She swallowed before going on. "How do you bounce back to normal life after something like that?"

Ethan sighed heavily. "How do you walk again after you've broken your leg?" he asked. "You focus on taking one step at a time until, suddenly, you're running." He shrugged. "Right now, the most important thing is the safety of those people out there, of you." He nodded towards her. "I'll think about running after we get this bastard."

Wiping another tear from her face, she nodded and took

the sweatshirt she'd been looking at. "I'm done in here." She walked towards the cashier. "Ethan?" She glanced over her shoulder.

"Yeah?" He tilted his head.

"Thanks."

The man smiled. It was one of the only times she'd witnessed him do so.

She sat in first class next to Blake as the plane carried them to his home. While he slept, she thought about their lives together. She loved acting and knew that, no matter what, it would always be a part of her future. She was thankful Blake didn't appear to have any issues with her work, unlike the last guy she'd dated, who had started complaining about her being in the spotlight more than he was after their fifth night together.

Rein had been a backup dancer for one of her favorite singers. She'd met him backstage at a concert and had been excited when he'd asked her out quickly. Maybe her experience with Rein was why she hadn't dated in the past two years?

When you were in the business, it was hard to date, let alone find someone that would stick around. She glanced over at Blake and knew without a doubt that he was the sticking kind.

By the time she landed, she had worked out her feelings towards Blake. The fact was, she'd never felt so strongly for anyone other than her sister, Claire. Love didn't come easy for her. Neither did trust. Sure, she had people she trusted to do jobs for her, and she trusted Amanda to handle her career, but those were simple tasks and friendships. And one thing was now very clear—she trusted Blake with everything, including her heart.

A huge limo picked them up at the airport and his

entire family shuffled into the car while Javan, Corey, and three more men who worked for Ethan filled two dark SUVs that flanked the limo.

"Wow, we're getting the royal treatment," Blake's father joked. The man was a surprise to her. She'd seen hundreds of images of his parents. His mother was just as pretty as she was in photos and his father, his dark hair now a light shade of silver, looked the same as well.

Still, Kenneth, who had requested that Robin call him Ken, was more easygoing than she'd expected a retired senator to be. Coleen, Blake's mother, was quieter than she'd expected. The woman looked worried and doted over Blake like he was the sole reason for her life.

Robin had never felt that kind of parental love before and standing on the outside watching it, she felt the flames of jealousy singe. What would it have been like if she and Claire had been raised in a loving home?

She was positive she and her sister were so close because that's all they had. Even when Robin had moved to California with their mother, and Claire had stayed in Colorado, the distance had only made them closer. The courts may have decided who lived with whom, but that didn't negate the girls' love and loyalty for one another.

She glanced over at his sister Ann, who was holding their youngest, Liam. The little dark-haired boy was five years old. His older sisters, Camilla, ten, and Cora, eight, were fast asleep, leaning on their father. Here it was again, another example of a perfect family full of love.

"Everything okay?" Blake asked her as he took her hand in his.

She glanced out the windows and noticed that they'd turned off the main highway.

"Yes," she answered. "Are we close?"

"Yeah, my parents' place is just around the corner." He motioned to the right side of the road. "I'm another few miles further."

"I'm looking forward to seeing your barndominium," she said, trying to lighten the quiet mood that filled the car.

"There used to be a home on the site," Coleen said with a smile. "It burned down about ten years ago, leaving only the barn. It was Blake's idea to turn the old thing into a home." She shook her head and chuckled. "I would have never thought that it would make such a wonderful place."

"You and me both," Ken added, taking his wife's hand in his. "It's sure nice having him so close. When he's in town, that is."

"Hey, I'm just thankful you kept your place in DC so I can use it when I'm there," Blake said to his father.

"That was my idea," Coleen added. Then she turned to Robin. "Where is home for you?"

"I have an apartment in San Diego," she answered.

"Is your family from San Diego?" Coleen asked her.

"N-no. My mother lives in LA with her boyfriend. My father is still back in Colorado," she answered as the limo slowed.

"Where in Colorado are you from?" Ken asked.

"Castle Rock. Well, I was there until I was fifteen. Then my parents divorced, and I was sent out to California with mom while my sister Claire stayed with dad."

The limo stopped in front of a beautiful two-story white stone home. Each window on the front had black shutters. The matching front door sat below a massive archway. The driveway circled the front of the home, and they stopped directly under the carport.

There were rows and rows of tulips in front of perfectly manicured bushes separating the home and the drive.

"You have a beautiful home," she said as they all climbed out of the limo.

"Thank you. Do the two of you have time to come in or are you wanting to head home and get some rest?" Coleen asked.

Robin glanced at Blake who was standing beside her. "I'm tired, Mom. Maybe we can do dinner tomorrow?"

Coleen walked over and hugged Blake. "I'll make your favorite dish," she said softly before kissing him on the cheek. "Go home. Get some rest."

They waited until his parents' luggage was unloaded and carried into the house before climbing back into the limo.

"I like your parents," she said when they were on their way.

"They like you," Blake said with a sigh.

"Hurting?" she asked.

"Tired." He pulled her close to his side. "And wanting to be home."

From there, they traveled another mile down the road and dropped Ethan, Ann, and their three kids, who had slept the entire drive, off at their home, which was similar to his parents' house. This one was made of dark stone and wood instead of white stones. It was a little newer looking, and just as impressive.

"They have another home in Washington State and spend their summers there close to Ethan's parents," Blake said as they drove away. "They spend their winters down here so the girls can go to school here."

From his sister's home, the limo turned down a gravel road with a split-rail wood fence on either side of them.

"This is all my land," Blake said, motioning to the fence. "There's just over twenty acres." Then he nodded. "Home."

She followed his gaze and gasped slightly. She'd seen plenty of pictures of the place, but none of them showed the sheer size of it. "It's massive." She leaned towards the window as the limo turned and parked in front of the two massive garage doors.

She stepped out of the limo and grabbed her backpack stuffed with her things and her new purchases. She followed him down a cement pathway through the massive, covered porch, which was filled with cozy-looking patio furniture, a porch swing, and several large potted ferns and flowers.

Blake punched in a code on the keypad next to large French doors and then opened them and stood back. "Welcome." He motioned for her to enter. She heard the limo driving away and watched the SUV park in front of the garage.

"Someone will be on duty twenty-four seven. Not to mention the... agents." He nodded slightly.

If everything was set, his entire place had already been wired and safeguarded by the FBI.

She stepped through the doors and was immediately in awe of the beauty of the space. There was a sitting area to the left where you would be able to remove dirty shoes, hang coats, or set packages down on the long bench that had cubbies underneath and hooks above.

The living room space was directly in the middle of the first space. A two-story stone fireplace filled the left wall beyond the bench and a cozy leather sofa and chair faced the fireplace. A huge flat-screen television sat over the mantel and there was a full bookshelf on the other side of the fireplace. A large kitchen island separated the two spaces. The ceiling over the kitchen was lowered, as there were rooms above that space. A dining area sat over to the side, and French doors much like the front doors led off to the back of the building. What appeared to be a laundry room and walk-in pantry sat on the other side of the kitchen.

"There's a guest bedroom through there," Blake said, motioning to a hallway, "for anyone who can't do stairs." He smiled and motioned towards the stairs that sat to the left of the front doors. "Our room's up there." He followed her up the stairs.

The posts were wood, and the railings were iron bars running horizontally. The look was unique and beautiful.

Immediately upstairs there was a loft area that held a comfortable chair surrounded by bookshelves.

"I couldn't bring the entire library with me," Blake said with a shrug. "But at least I have this space."

"I like it," she said, following him around the landing towards the back of the building just over the kitchen area.

"My office and a game room of sorts that way," Blake said, motioning to the opposite side. "The main bedroom is above the kitchen. Two guest rooms on that side and my office and game room on the other."

"I would have thought that your front door would've been on the end instead of in the middle of the barn," she said, following him to the double wood doors she imagined was the main bedroom.

"Yeah, this was a better design. I looked at a ton of different ways of doing things." He opened the door and stepped inside. "I liked this one the best."

She followed him inside and once again was in awe of the sheer size of the space. Cedarwood planks covered the entire ceiling of his room while soft gray wood planks covered his floor. Throughout the entire home, there were hints of wood, yet it wasn't overdone like most country homes she'd seen in magazines.

Blake walked in and set his backpack on a chair in the corner. Robin set hers down on the bed and walked around. French doors led out to a private covered balcony that overlooked a small pond. Through a set of sliding barn doors was the en suite bathroom. The bathtub was huge and sat directly below a frosted window through which sunlight was streaming in. The walk-in glass shower filled the opposite wall, with two sinks and counter space between.

"I like your home." She turned back to Blake, who had sat down and removed his shoes.

"I'll give you a tour later. I'm just too exhausted to move." He reached over and picked up a remote from the nightstand next to the bed. With the flick of his wrist, every blind in the room slid shut, sending the room into almost sheer darkness.

"Nice," she said, toeing off her shoes.

Blake stood and moved her bag to the chair next to his, pulled down the comforter, and crawled in fully clothed. When he patted the spot next to him, she removed her pants and bra, leaving her shirt and panties on, and crawled in beside him.

CHAPTER NINETEEN

B lake shifted and pain shot through his shoulder. Robin jerked awake next to him.

"Are you okay?" she asked as her hands gently moved over him.

"Just a twinge." He tried to pull her back to his side.

"Let me look. We're supposed to change the bandages..." She disappeared and reached for the light. He shut his eyes as the room lit up.

"You're bleeding through the bandages," she said, and he felt her weight leave the bed. "Come in the bathroom, I'll clean you up."

"I could go for a shower," he said, sitting up. Just seeing her standing in his bedroom in a T-shirt and underwear had his mouth watering. "You look amazing," he said quickly.

Robin laughed. "You must be delusional." She glanced down at herself. "My hair is a rat's nest, my clothes are..." She motioned to the T-shirt, which she'd purchased at the airport.

He walked slowly towards her and wrapped his arms

around her. "And yet." He pushed his desire against her hip and watched her eyes widen as she smiled up at him.

"I think I can help you out with that problem as well." She purred as she tugged him towards the bathroom.

Showering in his shower, with Robin's wet body pressed up against his, was one of his favorite moments of his life. She'd pulled off the soiled bandages, and he'd let the water run over his stitches while they'd enjoyed one another slowly.

After the shower, he'd sat still while she'd cleaned and rebandaged his shoulder. Since his head wound was a small cut over a huge bump, he'd opted to forgo the bandage.

"How are you feeling?" Robin asked him as they made their way downstairs. He'd pulled on a pair of sweatpants and had given her a pair of his to wear as well. She'd rolled up the legs and was wearing another T-shirt she'd purchased at the airport. He felt bad that all of her things had been destroyed in the blast. Maybe he should take her shopping in Atlanta tomorrow?

"I'll survive," he replied. "Hungry?"

"Starving." She sat down at the bar and watched as he pulled out some eggs and bread from the fridge. "Is that stuff still good?" she asked.

He set them on the counter near the stove. "Grocery delivery was yesterday morning."

"Oh. I would have never thought of that. Whenever I get home after a long trip, I always forget stuff like that. Then, after my power nap to get back on track at my time zone, I wake up starving and there's nothing in the house."

He chuckled. "The first few times I did that, I learned to set up delivery for the morning I return. Kim, the woman who cleans and watches out for the place while I'm gone, has been working for our family for over twenty years." He smiled. "You'll probably meet her tomorrow night." He stopped and glanced down at his phone, and frowned. "Scratch that, tonight, at my parents' place."

Robin's eyebrows jerked up. "It's tomorrow already?" She pulled out her phone, then looked outside at the dark windows and sighed. "It's two in the morning. I was just thinking it was around eight or nine at night."

He chuckled and pulled out a few pans. "Breakfast?" he asked. "I was thinking of making blueberry French toast, eggs, and bacon." He walked over and took the package of bacon from the fridge.

"That sounds great. What can I do to help?" she asked.

"Sit there. Keep me company. I like to cook," he threw over his shoulder as he got to work.

"Okay." She sighed behind him. "Well, first off I should probably confess to something."

He stopped what he was doing and held his breath as he waited for her next words.

"What?" he asked finally.

She smiled. "I don't like cooking," she finally said. He chuckled and turned back around.

"It's not for everyone," he admitted. "I fell in love with it when I stuck around the kitchens begging for food. One day Alice decided that, if I was going to be underfoot, I might as well help out." While he cooked, he told Robin of his time growing up in the château.

She talked briefly about living with her mother in California and how she'd moved out on her own the moment she could.

"Freedom," she said later, as she took a bite of eggs, "was something I needed for my sanity."

They sat at the bar instead of the table a few feet away since it was a little less formal. He always ate at the bar top when he was alone, so it just seemed natural to sit there with Robin.

"Is your mother that bad?" he asked her.

"Both of our parents are that bad. I don't know how Claire and I turned out any sort of normal."

"You had each other," he suggested. "Before... all the craziness in my childhood, the only rock-solid thing in my life was my sister. Even though we're ten years apart, she has always been there for me."

"I bet a lot of things changed after that time," she said, looking down at her plate.

He reached over and took her hand. "It will get better. I promise. After we catch this guy..."

"How do you know we will?" she asked, suddenly putting her fork down. "What if we spend the rest of our lives hiding? Jumping at shadows?" She closed her eyes and sat back. She shook her head, opened her eyes, and looked at him. "I can't—I won't put you through that."

He set his fork down, but instead of taking her hand, he nudged the barstool until she was turned towards him. Leaning closer to her, he gazed deeply into her eyes.

"I'm not running. If you tell me this"—he motioned between them— "is over because you've grown bored of me or... you hate me, then I'll let you go. But if you're trying to break this off because of some madman..." He shook his head and cupped her face in his hands gently. His heart broke a little seeing the tears slide from her eyes. Using his thumb, he wiped them away as quickly as they fell. "Then you'd better get used to seeing me around."

She smiled. Even though it was a weak smile, it made his heart skip.

"I love you," she said softly. At first, he'd thought he'd heard wrong, but then she said it again a little louder.

"I love you too," he said and kissed her. "Now, let's finish eating our breakfast so we can go back upstairs and fall asleep for a couple of hours while watching a movie and then wake up in time to go have dinner at my folks' place."

She laughed and picked up her fork again. "Sounds like a perfect day."

His well-laid plans would have worked if not for Ethan knocking on the door shortly before sunrise. Crawling out of bed, he checked the Ring doorbell and groaned into his phone when he saw Ethan standing there in the dark mist.

"Go away," he said to Ethan.

"Let me in," Ethan said quickly. "It's wet and cold out here."

"Wet? Cold?" Blake glanced at the phone and noticed the temperature was in the sixties and there was a dense fog warning. "It's spring in Georgia."

"Yeah, did I mention that it's cold and wet?" Ethan whined.

Chuckling, he unlocked the door and turned off the house alarm. Even though Ethan already knew the code to get in, his brother-in-law only used it in emergencies.

"Everything okay?" Robin asked as he crawled out of bed.

"Yeah, I'm sure he just wants to fill me in on what's going on." He pulled on his sweats again. "No." He stopped her from getting out of bed. "Stay. I'm sure it'll just be a few minutes."

She lay back down and pulled the covers up and closed her eyes. "Come back soon," she said as he left the room.

"What's up?" he asked when he stepped into the kitchen. Ethan was helping himself to a cup of coffee.

"Want one?" he asked, motioning with the cup.

"No, I plan on heading back to bed when you leave."

Ethan's eyes moved to the upstairs. "Robin sleeping still?"

"You're stalling," he said, crossing his arms over his chest. He knew his brother-in-law too well.

Ethan sighed. "We caught someone sneaking around a couple of hours ago."

"You did?" He straightened. "And?"

"He claims he just got lost, but he had a gun and enough ammo on him to take down a small army." Ethan sipped his coffee.

"But?" He knew the worried look Ethan had.

"Everyone thinks it's your guy," Ethan added.

"You don't?" he asked.

Ethan shrugged. "Doesn't matter what I think. The FBI is pulling out. They've taken him into custody and are closing the book."

Blake felt his stomach roll. "You don't think it's him?"

Ethan waited a moment then shook his head. "We're not going anywhere."

"Who was it?" Blake asked.

"His name is Michael Holt. He has no priors," Ethan answered.

"And?" he asked, knowing there was more behind why Ethan didn't think he was the guy.

"And Michael hasn't traveled outside the U.S. in the past year," Ethan added dryly.

He thought for a moment. "But the FBI thinks it's the guy?"

"They think he traveled using his brother's credentials," Ethan said.

"His brother?" He walked over and made himself a cup of coffee. He doubted that he could get back to sleep now anyway.

"Connor Holt," Ethan added. "Who was in Paris less than a week ago."

Blake glanced upstairs and thought about waking Robin to ask if she knew of either man.

"Yeah, I was hoping to ask Robin if she knew either man," Ethan said.

"I'll go wake her." He knew she wouldn't want to wait any longer for the information. Setting his mug down, he climbed the stairs. He was at the top landing when he heard the crash and scream.

Somehow, Ethan made it to the bedroom door at the same time he did.

He took in the empty bed, and the fact that one of the windowpanes on the French doors leading to his private balcony was smashed. He rushed forward.

As glass cut into his feet, he watched Ethan bolt through the opened door, his gun drawn.

CHAPTER TWENTY

Robin heard Blake and Ethan talking downstairs. Just the sound of the two men had her worrying and wondering what was going on.

She crawled out of bed and made her way to the bathroom to freshen up before heading down herself.

After cleaning up, she pulled on the jeans she'd worn the day before and found a sweatshirt in Blake's closet and pulled it on. She was just about to head downstairs when strong arms wrapped around her.

She screamed as she was picked up. She tried to fight back, but he was too strong. She could only scream and kick as he flew out the door into the cold morning.

Mist and darkness instantly engulfed them. Since she was barefoot, she tried to kick out, aiming for anything tender between the giant man's legs.

Her flailing around was as efficient as water on stone. The man ran fast, with her thrown over his shoulder. Each step he took knocked her breath from her since his shoulder was jammed into her gut.

Then she heard her name on the wind. Blake.

"Here!" she cried out, only to be tossed onto the hard ground. The dark figure cupped a hand over her mouth, and she did what she'd done in *Magnanimous*, in the scene where the supervillain had pinned her down. She bit the man's hand and didn't let go until she tasted blood. Only this time, the blood was real and not a strawberry flavored mixture.

She swiped at the face that hovered just out of sight with her fingernails. She wailed and cried out, repeatedly, once his beefy hand retreated.

She knew that at any moment, Blake or Ethan would be there, pulling her free. Saving her.

But the longer she fought, the more she worried the man had traveled too far away from them. That she'd lost her only hope somewhere in the dark mist.

She had to break free. To run. To get back to Blake. She continued to scratch with her fingernails and kick out with her bare feet.

Strong hands cupped her wrists and pulled her arms high over her head. She was shaken so hard that her eyes rolled, and her screams died in her throat.

Then everything stopped as she lay there, in the tall wet grass, looking at the dark figure looming over her.

"You're finally mine," the deep voice said, causing her entire body to shake. "And I'll never let anyone else ever touch you."

The mist seemed to curl around them, cocooning them in the grayness, blocking out all sights and sounds.

She tried to focus her eyes, to see the man that hovered over her, his weight cutting off her air supply, but her eyes wouldn't work. Nothing worked. Not even her voice. He'd shaken her so hard, so fast, that she was feeling dizzy and confused.

She felt him shifting over her, felt his weight getting heavier. Oh god, this was it. This was going to be the end of her. One way or another, she was going to die in this field.

Then a sound pierced the silence. The single-shot stopped everything. The dark figure above her stopped. He looked down at his chest and hands then back up into the darkness.

"You can't have her," he growled and moved to stand up. His weight lifted from her, allowing her to take in a deep breath. She screamed this time when another shot rang out directly above her head.

This time, the dark figure landed next to her with a deep thud as blood splattered her face and hair.

Then Blake was there, holding her, telling her that everything was going to be all right. She was gently lifted and carried back through the tall fresh grass, then laid gently on the sofa as blankets were wrapped around her.

Ethan handed Blake a fresh towel and stood there talking on the phone while Blake gently cleaned the blood from her.

"Shower," she managed to get out.

Blake glanced at Ethan, who nodded.

When Blake picked her up and started to carry her upstairs, she shook her head. "Down here is fine."

She didn't want to admit that it was too soon to return to the bedroom upstairs. She didn't want to see the broken glass. To know that moments earlier, she'd been fast asleep, happily snuggled up against Blake, unaware that danger was just outside.

Blake carried her down the hallway into the guest bathroom. When he set her on her feet, her legs gave out and his arms wrapped around her.

"My god," Blake said, holding onto her tightly.

"I'm okay," she said a couple of times, more to assure herself than him.

When he released her, Ethan knocked on the door.

"Better take some photos first," Ethan called out to Blake.

"Right." Blake nodded. "I know the drill," he said softly, then he sighed. "I need to take pictures." He motioned to her face and hair. "For Ethan's protection."

"He killed him?" she asked, feeling a little more centered.

"Yeah. We didn't think we were going to reach you in time," Blake said, pulling out his phone. "Hold still. Close your eyes if you want."

She did so while he snapped more than a dozen pictures of her from every angle. "Done," he said. He helped her peel off her ruined clothes.

When she stepped under the hot water, her legs melted and buckled. Blake was there, fully clothed, to catch her.

"I need..." she cried out, covering her face with her hands as the blood washed from her hair and face.

"I've got you," he said, setting her on the bench, adjusting the spray, and then gently washing her with soap.

She sat there, crying and blocking out everything except for the gentle way Blake touched her. He pulled her up into his arms. He'd removed his clothes at some point.

When they stepped out of the shower, Ethan called out. "The police are here. They'd like to talk to the pair of you."

"Give us a minute," Blake called out.

"I put some fresh clothes outside the door," Ethan added. "There's a female officer here to talk to Robin."

"My name is Kate. I'm here when you're ready," a friendly female voice called out.

"Thank you," Robin said with a slight sob.

Blake brought in the clothes and once again she pulled on a pair of sweats. This pair fit her almost perfectly.

"I'm sure they belong to my sister," Blake said with a smile as he pulled on a pair of jeans and a shirt. "I'll bet you my entire family is out there as well."

Sure enough, when they stepped back into the living room, his family was there along with five police officers. Two of them were women, who sat with Robin as she told them exactly what had happened.

She was handed a cup of coffee just as the rain outside started falling harder and faster. She'd never been to Georgia before, but since no one in the room seemed to be concerned about the rate the water was falling outside, she tried not to be either.

Just hearing the name of the first man they'd caught outside a few hours ago gave her shivers. Since they were still trying to identify the second, they weren't positive of his name. Ethan seemed to think it was Connor Holt. He was positive the men were brothers.

But why would the brothers go after her? The question kept circling in her head while she answered all the police questions, sometimes two or three times.

She was taken into the guest room, her growing bruises photographed by the female officer and even measured.

The rain continued to fall hard for about fifteen minutes and was gone as quickly as it came. By the time the police left, the sun was shining outside.

Coleen and Ann were in the kitchen making breakfast while the kids, who were brought down from one of the guest rooms upstairs where they'd been sleeping since they'd arrived, sat on the sofa and watched cartoons.

She had to admit, watching the silly antics helped push the darkness away. Her eyes kept returning to the children.

Hearing their laughter and seeing the happiness in their eyes was... therapeutic.

Blake sat by her the entire time, his hand in hers. Medics had come and removed a few shards of glass from his feet when they'd looked at her.

"Breakfast is ready," Coleen said. The kids sprang up from the sofa and rushed to the table.

"They're animals," Blake said with a smile. "Are you okay?"

She took a deep breath before nodding. "This is helping." She nodded to the kids.

"Yeah, the rug rats are good for some things." Blake chuckled. "Hungry?"

She thought about it for a moment, then nodded. "I could eat."

She stood up and slowly made her way across the room, moving like a zombie. It took all her energy, and she frowned as she sat down.

"It'll take some time," Blake said quietly as he sat next to her at the table. "Eat. Then we'll rest."

She had never had homemade butter pecan waffles before. When she'd sat down, she'd doubted she would be able to finish one, let alone two of them.

"My mom learned a few things from Alice as well," Blake said, motioning with his fork to the waffles.

"Those were wonderful," she admitted, setting down her fork. "Thank you all for being here."

Just then, Robin's cell phone rang from somewhere in the house. Her eyes moved upstairs.

"I'll go get it." Blake jumped up and ran up the stairs. Everyone was quiet until he came back down and handed her the phone.

Looking at the screen, she felt tears pool in her eyes. "My sister."

"We'll clean up and then get out of your hair," Ethan said, his eyes going to Blake, who nodded in response.

"We can stay down here in this room," Blake told her. "Why don't you head in, call Claire back. I'll be in soon."

She stood she made her way to the guest room down the hallway. This room was just as nice as Blake's room, if just a little smaller. The bed was a queen instead of an oversized king.

She sat on it, pulled the throw blanket over her shoulders, and called Claire.

"Are you okay?" Claire answered on the first ring.

"I'm..." Tears rolled down her cheeks. "Fine." The word burst from her.

"It's all over the news. You were kidnapped?" Claire asked.

"I was... but Blake and Ethan... they came and..." The rest of the story flew from her in one long run-on sentence. She gulped air between sobs. She didn't even know if Claire understood anything she was saying since it was all garbled together. When she was done, she wiped her eyes with the back of her hand.

"You're okay," Claire said softly. "I can cut my trip short and head there?"

"No," Robin said, knowing that her sister's trip to Italy was a once-in-a-lifetime dream. Whereas Robin dreamed of being in the spotlight, Claire's dream was to study from some of the best fashion designers.

Robin didn't want to tell her sister that it was foolish, since Claire was far better than them already, but she wasn't going to take this dream away. Not since she knew that

Claire had just arrived in Italy the day before the bombing. She'd had to convince her then not to cut her trip short. But now it was Robin who'd been targeted instead of Blake.

By the time Blake came into the room, Robin felt a little steadier, thanks to Claire's calming voice.

"Everything okay?" Blake asked, sitting next to her on the bed.

"Yes." She glanced towards the television. "Claire says it's all over the news."

"Want to…" He motioned to the set.

"No." She turned to him. "I'd rather crawl in bed and drop off for a few more hours."

He smiled. "I was thinking the same thing."

"How are your feet?" she asked as they crawled under the covers together.

"They're fine. How are you?" He pulled her closer.

"Sore, but alive. Thanks to you and Ethan." She closed her eyes and laid her head on his chest. Just hearing his heart beating steadily had her relaxing even more.

"I'll always be there for you." His hand rubbed her shoulder. "I was scared."

She nodded. "So was I."

"I know it's early, but I was thinking… how'd you like to move in with me?" Blake asked.

She glanced up at him and smiled. "Isn't that what this is?"

His lips curved up. "I mean…"

Leaning up, she placed her lips over his. "I know what you meant."

He chuckled. "Okay, is that a yes?"

She nodded. "I was growing tired of my apartment anyway," she said with a sigh, resting her head back down.

"You may change your mind after I have a few trips to Washington," Blake said with a sigh.

"We have a few trips you mean?" she said holding in a yawn. "As you said, I'll always be there for you."

Blake's arms tightened for a moment around her. "I love you."

"I love you too." She drifted off, totally relaxed and knowing she was safe.

CHAPTER TWENTY-ONE

Over the next week, more and more details were brought to light. The first was that Ethan had killed Connor Holt in the field. The second was that it had been Connor who had been in Paris.

It was confirmed, however, that the threatening messages Robin had been receiving for the past year were from the brother's computer.

The rest was still gray. There was no proof that Connor had gotten his hands on a gun and shot at them, nor was there proof that it had been Connor who had set the explosive.

Between Ethan and Blake, they believed the man was much larger than the shadow that had been spotted on the security cameras.

Connor stood six-foot-five and weighed two-twenty. The figure in black on the security camera appeared much smaller and a hell of a lot leaner. Which made them think of Michael, Connor's younger brother.

In the men's home back in LA, they found a massive shrine to Robin. The entire apartment was filled with photos, news articles, and even some of her objects, which the police claim had been purchased off an auction site.

"Two brothers' secret obsession," the news was calling it. "How had two mechanics come to hunt down a Hollywood elite?" The media was obsessed with the story.

They couldn't turn on the television without someone talking about it. It had taken Robin a few days before she'd finally returned to the upstairs room.

The day after, he'd replaced the broken glass in the door.

Amanda flew out that following day and brought two large suitcases of Robin's own clothing from her apartment. Her friend only stayed a day but assured them that the rest of Robin's things were being packed up and delivered there.

Having her friend there seemed to help her even more out of the darkness. As did having his sister and her kids in the house.

They were all sitting on the sofa, watching cartoons one evening, when he got a call from his office. For the past week, since the kidnapping, he'd tried to handle as much of his work as he could while Robin was sleeping.

"Sorry," he said to the room. He answered the call as he headed up the stairs.

"You thought you could escape me?" the raspy voice hissed into the phone. "Don't think I don't know that it was your fault she got hurt. Those brothers have no clue the length I'll go to protect her." Blake stopped walking and glanced around. He caught Ethan's eyes, His brother-in-law stood up and rushed to his side. They both listened while the voice continued. "She's my guardian angel and I'm hers and you are nothing!" The voice had risen to a scream.

Now, Robin was beside him and the television was quiet as everyone watched him.

"What do you want?" Blake asked.

"Your head on a platter," the voice said before he hung up.

"Well, shit," Ethan said, running his hands through his hair. "I'd hoped..." He shook his head.

Blake pulled Robin into his arms and held on.

"It's not over," she said, and he felt her crying.

His heart sank just hearing her concern. He wasn't upset or worried for himself. This was breaking her. How could they survive after this? They'd barely survived the brothers. Now, there was still a madman out there after him.

"He's the one," Ethan said, pulling out his phone. "The shooter and the one who set the bomb. I guarantee it." He stepped into Blake's office to make some calls.

Blake took Robin back downstairs and held her while they waited to find out their next moves.

"What do we do now?" Robin asked him softly as the kids went back to watching television.

"Now"—he squeezed her shoulders— "we wait and stay together."

"That was always in the plans." She smiled up at him. "We could go away again?"

He thought about taking her to some secluded island in the Pacific. Somewhere warm, somewhere it would be only the two of them. But he knew that wasn't possible. No matter where they went, they wouldn't be safe.

"I know," she said before he could answer.

Ethan came rushing down the stairs a moment later. "News," he said to Ann, who turned the channel to the news station she worked for.

"Once again, there's been an explosion down at the

capitol building," the news anchor said as scenes of fire and mayhem filled the screen.

"My office." Blake stood up. "I..."

"Sit," Ethan said. "You have to stay put. The FBI is on its way here again. For now, we all have to stay put."

Within the hour, his parents and the FBI arrived, and his home was once again filled with people all talking at once. Ethan and Javan were working with the FBI agent, Thomas Bruns, who had been in charge last time. His parents quietly worked with the kids at the table, doing their homework or coloring.

Robin sat beside him, quietly listening to it all, a concerned look in her eyes. One thing was sure. Whatever happened now, he was going to spend the rest of his life making sure she felt safe wherever they went.

From the news, they found out that three bodies had been found so far in the blast. Thankfully, since it was so late in the evening, most of the employees had already gone home for the night.

A woman's body was found in the rubble of his office, which the news was claiming was Leslie Cooper. The body of a janitor named Carl Bell was found just outside in the hallway, and a male's body was discovered in the office directly above his.

A lawyer by the name of Marcus Colt worked upstairs. A few others in the building were injured but nothing too serious. They were still searching for survivors and bodies.

This explosion was twice the size of the one at the château. The building would most likely have to be condemned, or so the news was saying. Images of him and Leslie flashed on the screen. He was having a difficult time processing all of it. If he hadn't been staying with Robin,

Leslie would have probably been home instead of at the office.

He'd neglected his work in the past week and both Leslie and Jeffery were having to help carry the load.

"Shit," he sighed, catching a few people's attention. "My other PA. Jeffery Maguire. Is there any word on him?" he asked the agent.

Thomas glanced down at his pad as he wrote Jeffery's name. "We'll look into it. Do you happen to have his number?"

Instead of giving it to the agent, Blake dialed the man directly. Jeffery answered on the second ring.

"You're safe," Blake said with a sigh.

"Yes, I stepped out to get us some coffee," Jeffery said, and Blake could hear the sirens in the background. "I'm still here with the police giving my statement."

"Good." Blake relaxed.

"Leslie…" Jefferey's voice cracked.

"I know." He sighed. "Let me know if you need anything," he said before hanging up.

"Anyone else in your office?" the agent asked.

"No, the rest were working from home while I was out this week," he answered. "When I stay home, I think it's only fair that they get to as well. Leslie and Jeffery were the exceptions. Both wanted to keep working from the office." He laid his head in his hands. "Rumors were, after Paris, they had a… thing for one another."

Robin squeezed his arm. Somehow that thought made everything worse. Hadn't he come close to losing Robin days ago? What would he do if things hadn't turned out the way they had? Or worse, what would she do if something happened to him?

Once again, thoughts of taking Robin away from this all played in his head.

Then Ethan pulled him aside. "How long has Jeffery Maguire worked for you?"

Blake thought about it for a moment. "About three years. Why?" When Ethan gave him a look, he felt his gut twist. "Jeffery?" he asked as he shook his head.

Ethan's eyebrows rose. "He's the right build. Had access to both the château and your office. Not to mention, he knew where you were the night of the shooting."

"But... Jeffery hasn't..."—he glanced towards Robin—"shown anything but kindness."

Ethan nodded. "Yeah, fits."

Blake closed his eyes and thought about it for a moment. "He's been my assistant for three years," he reiterated.

"And things started going crazy after you met Robin. If he's had a secret thing for her... then you come in and sweep her off her feet. It fits," Ethan said quietly.

It did fit. The more he thought about it, the more it made sense. "Okay, so we tell..."

"No. If the FBI goes rushing in, he might not have anything to incriminate him. From what I know of the guy, he's smart," Ethan said, and Blake nodded in agreement.

"It's one of the reasons I hired him. Top of his class, graduated with honors, blah, blah, blah." He looked over to Robin.

"Okay, so we play it cool," Ethan said with a nod. "Until my team can do some recon." He started to walk away, but Blake stopped him.

"What do you need from me?"

Ethan smiled and winked. "Nothing, kid, just let us GI Joes do our thing."

Blake laughed. "You're never going to let me forget that, are you?"

Ethan laughed. "Never." He motioned to Javan, and the pair left.

"What was that all about?" Robin asked when he sat down beside her.

"I'll explain later," he said softly and took her hand in his.

Enough pizza to feed an army was delivered an hour later. His nieces and nephews were shuttled back to their home along with his sister and parents.

"Why blow up your office when you weren't there?" Robin asked when they were finally alone again, except for the half dozen or so agents stationed around his home.

"I had a call earlier to go in. I blew it off," he admitted, not wanting to tell her that it was Jeffery that had demanded he be there for a late meeting. So many other things were clicking into place.

The more he thought about it, the more ironic it was. After all, all those years ago, it had been his father's assistant who had kidnapped him and almost killed his father.

When the threats had started, why hadn't he started looking among his people? Maybe because Ethan and his team had done background checks on everyone, and he knew for a fact that Jeffery was squeaky clean.

What would make a man go from one of the best personal assistants to a madman setting bombs and killing his coworker? And for what? Had he ever shown any interest in Robin?

Suddenly, nothing made sense.

"Are you going to let me in on what has that little crease between your eyebrows?" Robin asked, motioning to the spot.

"I could use a long hot shower," Blake said with a wink. Standing up, he took her hand and led her up the stairs.

He could tell she was a little irritated that he hadn't answered her question, so he put his finger over his lips, and she nodded.

He stepped into the bathroom, shut the door, and turned on the shower. Then he turned on the bathroom sink as well. When he leaned against the counter, she moved to stand in front of him.

"Has my PA Jeffery said anything to you?" he asked in a low tone.

Now it was Robin's turn to frown and reply in a whispered voice, "What do you mean by said anything to me? We chatted a few times, but..." Her eyes grew wide. "You think..." He watched her face pale.

CHAPTER TWENTY-TWO

"What are you going to do?" Robin whispered once the buzzing in her head had stopped. During filming, Blake's PA had been around. He'd given her attention, much like anyone else that met her. She'd known the man was starstruck from the first moment. She'd been flattered and then slightly annoyed when he'd hung around her a little too much.

For that matter, Leslie had been the same way towards her. But she'd been a little more relaxed around her than Jeffery.

But she'd told herself both were around because Blake was around, and she wasn't going to do anything to jeopardize their relationship. So she'd pushed her discomfort to the back of her mind.

"From the scared look on your face, he has said or done something to make you uncomfortable," Blake answered.

"Not... really. He was just always around. But then again, so were you," she pointed out.

"True. He and Leslie were always shadowing me."

"Do you think it's him? I thought you said he and Leslie

were seeing each other? Why would he blow her up?" she asked, feeling her gut twist.

"Why does any madman do what he does?" Blake sighed.

She nodded. "Okay, so what do we do now?"

"We?" Blake smiled. "We do nothing. Now, we let Ethan and his team go to work."

"What about the FBI?" she asked.

"For now, Ethan wants to handle this." He glanced around the room, which had quickly filled with steam. "How about we enjoy that?" he said, starting to remove his clothes.

The warmth was nice, so she peeled off her clothes and joined him. As they showered together, she filled Blake in on every detail, every encounter she could remember with Jeffery, both in Paris and at the château. There wasn't a lot, since she'd been busy with work and with Blake.

Still, enough that she too saw the pattern and figured that Jeffery had access and motive enough.

Knowing that the Holt brothers had been responsible for the threats sent to her while someone else threatened Blake, she could finally separate the two situations in her mind, which helped clear up a lot.

If the Holt brothers had been the ones calling her and harassing her for the past year, then whoever had threatened Blake had only started after that first night they'd met in Paris. After the picture of them, the one she loved and that was now the screen saver on her phone, had been published.

"Wasn't Jeffery with you that first night?" she asked as they dried off and dressed for bed.

Blake thought back and frowned. "No, Leslie was that

night. She'd been excited and had even tried to hang on my arm when we'd entered the party. Like it was a date instead of a work thing. I quickly set her straight before we were photographed," Blake answered. "The last thing I wanted was for rumors to go around that I was with an employee. My father..."

"I know all about your father's reputation," Robin jumped in. "Before he met your mother, that is," she added, earning a smile from Blake.

"They're good together," he said softly.

"So are we." She wrapped her arms around him. "Enough talk for tonight." She lifted on her toes and kissed him. "Let's go to bed."

Lying in Blake's arms as the sounds of the crickets outside the windows soothed her to sleep, she thought about everything.

She could grow to overcome the fear from what had happened to her in the past weeks. She tried very hard to convince herself of that. The police counselor she'd talked to after the kidnapping had talked to her about the PTSD and anxiety that would come after. She'd suggested Robin set up counseling. Blake had agreed to attend as well.

She remembered the conversation they'd had when they first met about him going to years of counseling after his ordeal as a child. Obviously, it had helped him.

Determined to set something up in the morning, she finally drifted off to a dreamless slumber.

She woke alone in the bed to the sound of more rain.

"Spring in Georgia," Blake said from the bathroom doorway.

She opened an eye and then sat up. "You're dressed. Dressed, dressed," she said, motioning to his suit and tie.

"Yes, I've arranged for a news conference down at the

site of the explosion," he answered. Before he finished talking, she was out of bed, her arms around him.

"No," she said, holding onto him.

He sighed and held onto her. "It's not really up to me. The FBI thinks…"

"I don't care what they think. You can't go." She closed her eyes. Blake's chuckle had her pulling back and glaring at him. "I mean it. I won't—"

Blake cupped her face. "I can't hide for the rest of my life," he said softly. "Ann and the kids are going to be here soon." He brushed his lips across hers.

"Why didn't you tell me this last night?" she asked.

"I only set it up this morning around two when I woke up to a dozen or more messages on my phone requesting interviews. I wanted you to get as much sleep as you could." He kissed her again. "Don't hate me," he said against her lips.

"Never." She closed her eyes and enjoying the feeling of him for a moment. "I can be dressed—"

"No." He pulled away. "You're going to stay here, where it's safe. Javan is downstairs making you his famous Brazilian breakfast." He lowered his voice. "Which consists of eggs, bacon, and the grease from an entire pig." He smiled. "Take your time getting dressed. I'd like you to watch the interview at nine."

She nodded and glanced over at the clock. "Two hours." She sighed and he nodded.

"Good luck. Stay safe." She held onto him again.

"You too." He kissed the top of her head. "I love you." He started to move away, then returned and kissed her more deeply. "When I get back, I'm going to try and convince you to marry me," he said with a smile. "I know it's only been—"

"Yes," she broke in with a smile. "Who cares if we've only known each other a month. When it's right..."

"It's right," he answered, then he kissed her. "Later," he promised, and then he left.

When she was alone, she did a little circle dance and grabbed a change of clothes, and went in to shower.

An hour later, when she finally made it downstairs, she realized Blake hadn't been kidding. There was enough grease on her plate to clog any heart. Javan's idea of bacon was thick slices of greasy ham coated in butter, scrambled eggs with butter, and large round rolls, which were... coated in butter.

Still, she slid some egg and ham in the roll and nibbled on the food as she sipped her coffee and watched the television set with Ann.

"Why aren't you up there?" Javan asked Ann. "Or don't you like getting in front of the camera any longer?"

Robin could tell that it was a tease since Ann smiled happily as she flipped the man off.

"I took family time," Ann said to her.

Deciding to take her mind off the waiting, she leaned forward. "Is it true the two of you met in Brazil?"

Javan laughed loudly and, as Robin and the kids all listened, he told everyone the story of how a haggard blonde woman in a brightly colored feathered headdress and no shoes arrived at his door one night with Ethan.

"Up until that moment," Ann broke into Javan's story, "I thought your father's name was Nathan." She smiled. "Your grandfather hired him to protect me."

"And it was a good thing too," Javan added. "With the mess you had gotten yourself into trying to expose the drug cartel."

Robin had heard the story. Or at least she thought she

had. What she hadn't heard was how Ann had convinced her camera crew to go into favelas, a part of town known for its huts and drug activity. As she listened, she realized that Ann had more balls than she would ever have.

Being able to sit face-to-face with some of the hardest of criminals took guts. Either that or pure stupidity. Which is how she felt about Blake holding a news conference.

"Which is why I now sit comfortably behind the camera." Ann squeezed her son, who was sitting in her lap, and kissed his head.

"Oh, look, there's your uncle now. Why don't the three of you head into the game room and color?" Ann said, setting her son down. "Camilla, please make sure you watch after your brother."

The dark-haired ten-year-old girl took Liam's hand as Cora, the eight-year-old, followed behind.

"I like your kids," Robin said absently as they all shifted to stand in front of the television while the police chief introduced Blake. The entire group was hidden under several large black umbrellas since the front of the building was gone now and offered no cover.

"Thank you all for your good wishes and concerns. My heart goes out to all of the family and friends of those who were affected by last night's tragedy," Blake started. "To answer a few questions, no, I wasn't anywhere near the building last night."

"What about Robin Stein?" someone shouted.

"Robin wasn't either," he answered quickly and then moved on. She knew what the press had wanted. They wanted to know her whereabouts. If she was okay after the kidnapping. But Blake hadn't given them anything. Then the camera panned out and Robin gasped when she noticed Jeffery Maguire standing just to Blake's left, behind him. On the other side, Ethan stood, looking formidable.

Why would they allow the man to get so close to Blake if they thought he was the one responsible for everything? Was it a trap? Why had Blake left her out of the plans once more?

She took a step forward, so focused on the man behind Blake that she didn't pay attention to what Blake was saying.

When Blake stepped out of view of the camera and the chief of police was back answering questions, she moved over and sat down.

"He risked his life for that?" Ann said with a shake of her head. "Sometimes I just don't understand men." She walked towards the stairs and disappeared up them, no doubt to check on her kids.

"This time, it wasn't his idea," Javan said to her once they were alone.

"It wasn't?" she asked, feeling frustrated.

"The FBI set it up. They were hoping…" Javan started.

"To put a target on his forehead," she finished. "I figured as much. I could tell he didn't seem too pleased leaving this morning."

"They think that he needs to show strength," Javan said.

"What do you think?" she asked.

"I think the two of you need to go to some remote island —I know a few by the way—and sit back until Ethan and I can catch this bastard," Javan added.

She smiled. "I like you, Javan."

The man laughed. "I like you too. Which is good because it seems like you're going to be sticking around."

She smiled. "I plan on it." She turned her eyes back to the television set, where reporters were shouting questions at the police chief. A question was asked of Blake, and the chief stepped back, allowing Blake to use the microphone to answer.

One minute Blake was standing there, the next the cameras were moving all around as people ran and ducked. Umbrellas were dropped and rain splattered the camera lens, distorting the images it showed.

"It appears there's been some sort of attack," the reporter said several times.

Robin jumped up and gasped as she watched the chaos. Then the scene changed to the reporter sitting behind a desk, looking confused.

"It appears that Senator Rhodes is down," the anchor said. "We are waiting for more details." She stopped and listened to her headset for a moment. "Yes, we are being told he's down. We will continue to bring information as we have it."

"Ann!" Javan called out.

Blake's sister rushed from the playroom and looked over the balcony. Her eyes flew to the set. They had switched back to the scene where Ethan was shielding Blake with his body. There was too much confusion to see what was happening, if Blake was hurt or not.

"We've got to go," Javan said to her. "You okay here?" he said to Ann.

"We're right behind you," she said, then she turned to the room upstairs. "Kids, let's go."

She grabbed her rain jacket and followed Javan out of the house. She stopped suddenly when a dark figure came out from the rain, lifted a gun, and shot Javan square in the chest. The man's massive body fell backward and landed in the mud with a thud.

Robin screamed, then took a step towards Javan to help

him. At no point did she think to run or hide. All she could think about was Blake and Javan, bleeding, dying.

"So, we're finally alone." The raspy voice had her looking up.

"L-Leslie?" Robin's head spun when she noticed the blonde step forward. "I... thought you were dead?" she asked, totally confused.

Leslie chuckled. "You're not the only one who can act." She sighed as her eyes ran over her. "I told him I'd keep you safe." Leslie started to move forward but Robin held up her hands and took a step back.

"How..." She glanced around. Surely there were FBI agents around still, right? They wouldn't have all gone with Blake to the city. Right?

"I made a call to an old friend and asked her to meet me in the office; Carena always did have a thing for me," Leslie said with a shrug. "Then I sent Jeffery off on a fool's errand to get coffee before she arrived." She smiled. "I worked explosive disposal during my time in the Marines." Leslie took another step towards her as Robin took one back.

Everything she knew about the woman could have filled one paragraph. She hadn't even known she'd been ex-military. "Why?" she asked, trying to catch up.

Leslie's eyes ran over her. "I would think that's obvious. I've been a huge fan of yours for years. When I saw you and wonder boy meet, something just..." Leslie placed the gun to the side of her head and smiled, showing the madness within. "Snapped." The gun moved back down as Leslie's eyes grew big. "Oh, no." She held up her free hand. "You don't have to be afraid of me. I would never hurt you," she said in a softer voice. "I'm here to save you." She shook her head. "Just like you said." She straightened. "Only heroes can save one another from the darkness."

Leslie's crazy smile was back. "Now..." She waved her gun towards the garage. "Let's go."

Before she could take another step, they were both surrounded, and Robin was yanked backward, back into the house. The door slammed shut and she was shoved behind the sofa as a heavy body covered hers.

"What..." She was gasping for air.

"I've got you." It was then that she realized that it was Blake holding onto her.

CHAPTER TWENTY-THREE

———————————

"You're here," Robin gasped and held onto him. "How?" She cried big fat tears that rolled down her cheeks as shouts sounded outside the door. They both jumped when several shots rang out and the glass in the front door exploded. More shots and then it grew silent.

"I think it's over," Blake said, looking down at Robin, who looked up at him with confusion. "Shall we go and see?"

"All clear!" someone called out.

"There you two are." Javan's face appeared, hovering over the sofa. "Are you going to come out or do you need a room?" The man chuckled.

"What the... what?" Robin touched her head. "I'm concussed. I must be."

Blake smiled at her. "No, just..." He frowned. "Plans changed after I left." He sat up and helped her up as well. "I wanted to call, but... there wasn't time." He sighed and instantly felt bad as Robin walked over and sat on the sofa. Ann came rushing down the stairs, holding Liam in her arms while Camilla and Cora hugged Ann's legs.

"What the hell!" Ann said, her eyes showing anger. "You stupid fools. You could have warned us." She turned and searched the room. "Where's my idiot husband?"

"Here," Ethan said, stepping inside. His brother-in-law was wearing all black over his Kevlar vest. Much like the one Blake wore under his suit now.

Ann walked over to her husband and hugged him, squeezing Liam in the middle. The girls rushed forward and held onto Ethan's legs.

He turned back to Robin, who was frowning at him even more. "This... was a plan?"

"Not mine." He held up his hands, then pointed to Ethan.

"Tattletale," Ethan said, earning him a slug on the shoulder from Ann.

"Was it Leslie?" Robin asked, looking into her hands. "That shot at you, that blew up the château and your office?"

He wrapped his arms around her shoulders. "Yes. She shot at me the first time in Paris and set both explosives. Ethan discovered it last night after he left. Things just weren't adding up about Jeffery. He had zero experience with guns or explosives. But Leslie..." He sighed. "Which didn't make sense if she'd perished in the explosion last night. That's why Ethan had the body that was discovered looked at more closely. It took most of the night, but finally, first thing this morning, right after I left, they discovered it wasn't Leslie. They still haven't identified who..."

"Her name is Carena," Robin broke in. "Or so Leslie said."

Blake looked over at Ethan, who nodded and let his family go to step outside.

"Once we knew for sure it wasn't Leslie, we set the trap.

Thanks to our connections at the local news." He smiled over at his sister who frowned back at him. We filmed the scene an hour ago and they played it as if it was a live feed instead."

"But someone shot at you today," Robin said as Ann and the kids moved over to sit on the sofa.

"Nope, we faked it." Blake smiled. "By the way, we owe Marcus. A lot." He chuckled. "He's the one that suggested we smoke out whoever was after me."

"Why?" Ann asked.

"We didn't know when Leslie would make a move. We hoped the false attack would force her to move up her time-line. The theory was that the Holt brothers pissed her off when they came after Robin," Blake explained, his eyes moving back over to Robin, who was looking at him. "And if someone else came after me..."

"So, you decided to scare the..." Ann glanced over at her children, who were watching them very closely. "Scare the birds out of us," she finished with a sigh.

"Do I have birds in me too, Mommy?" Liam asked quickly.

"We all do, honey," Ann said, hugging her son.

"That wasn't supposed to happen. We were supposed to be able to sneak in here before the bit aired, but it was too late when they spotted Leslie making her move," Blake answered, feeling guilty. "Since we figured Leslie had been listening to Ethan and Javan's radio chatter, we had to keep quiet. We suspected she had a mirror of my phone since she had plenty of access. We couldn't chance to contact anyone." He took Robin's hands, willing her to understand. "When we found out for sure that it was Leslie, we had to move quickly."

The door opened and Ethan and Agent Bruns walked

in. "It's all clear," Agent Bruns said. "Is everyone all right in here?" he asked us a couple more agents stepped inside.

"Yes, thanks," Blake answered. "Looks like I need to invest in some more glass," he joked as they stepped over the shards on the ground.

"Maybe some bulletproof stuff. I know a guy," Javan said, earning everyone's attention.

"I saw you get shot," Robin said, looking at the man.

Javan smiled and opened his jacket. "Kevlar, never leave home without it." He smiled as he rubbed his chest. "Hurts like a bitch but does the job." He closed his jacket. "Sorry to scare you. At such a close range, it knocked the wind out of me. I guess I'm not as young as I used to be."

"I've been telling you that for years," Ethan joked as he slapped Javan on the shoulder. "I'm beat." He turned to Ann. "How about we stop off and grab some pizza..." All three of his kids exploded with cheers as Ethan smiled and lifted Liam from Ann's arms. "Later," he said as the family left out the garage door.

"What happed to Leslie?" Robin asked the agent.

Part of Blake already knew, but he was surprised when agent Burns answered. "We've taken her into custody. She may have been a Marine, but she couldn't shoot the side of a barn standing a foot away. Explosives were her thing." The agent chuckled. "Luckily, my guys are better. She'll walk with a limp for a while. For now, we have her full confession on record. She'll be charged with domestic and international terrorism."

"Thanks," Blake responded. "What do you need from us?"

"Nothing. We'll be out of your hair soon enough," Agent Bruns said. "We're removing our equipment now." He turned to go. "Oh, nice performance this morning," he said with a smile. "You might want to plan on going on camera and letting everyone know you're alive."

Blake smiled. "I pre-recorded a message before coming here." For Robin's benefit, he added, "I plan on lying low for a while."

As they waited, they watched his message on the news that he was okay and that he'd be making another announcement tomorrow. It took less than an hour before the house was empty again. Once they were alone, Blake took Robin's hand and pulled her into his arms.

"How about a walk?" he suggested. "You haven't gotten to see a lot of the land."

She smiled up at him. "I'd like that."

He helped her pull on her raincoat and zipped his own, then took her hand and started out the back door. When he stepped outside, the rain had lightened to only a drizzle.

"Spring in Georgia." He smiled. "Tomorrow it will be in the high eighties," he said as they made their way towards the pond.

"It's beautiful here," Robin said, matching his pace.

"You should see it in the fall." He motioned to all the large trees surrounding the lake. "Everything turns bright red and orange."

"I'd like to. See it in the fall," she added with a smile.

They stopped at the end of the small dock he'd built two summers ago, and he turned to her.

"I'm sorry about... everything. Dragging you into my crazy," he started, but she stopped him by placing a hand over his lips.

"We both dragged one another into our own version of crazy," she said with a smile. "I'm just thankful you didn't take off running."

"Not a lot of people would stick through something like

what we went through in the past month," he agreed. She smiled.

"There might be crazier ahead," she suggested.

"We'll deal with it, together." He brushed his lips across hers. "If you'd like."

"I would." She smiled, then leaned back. "I discovered a lot about myself in the past few weeks."

"Oh?"

She nodded. "In the face of danger, I don't run and hide," she said. He smiled down at her. "I like homemade waffles more than I should," she added as he laughed. "And I want at least three kids."

This one stopped his heart. "Marry me," he said, his voice going low. "No doubt any of your Hollywood writers could pen a better proposal than that, but right now, all I can think of is starting our lives together."

Her smile slipped as tears rolled down her cheeks. "I doubt anyone could have written it better." She smiled. "Yes, I'll marry you." She kissed him as the sunlight broke through the clouds above them.

EPILOGUE

R obin stood at the stove as waffle batter splattered the apron she wore. She was pretty sure there was even some of it caked in her hair.

In the last week, they'd found out plenty more about Leslie. First, it had been discovered that Carena had been killed almost two days before the explosion, despite what Leslie had hinted at.

The next thing was that Carena had an old restraining order out for Leslie after the woman had spent three years stalking her while they'd served in the services together. It was one of the reasons Leslie had been discharged from the Marines a few months early.

Lastly, the FBI tied a few of those crazy emails Amanda had received for Robin to Leslie's computer, dating back two years. There were some from the brothers as well, but a lot of them were from her.

The emails talked about love and wanting to be with Robin and protect her from the world. They mentioned taking her away and hiding her from the eyes of others. Just reading through a handful of them made Robin understand why Amanda had kept them from her.

It had just been fate that she'd gotten a job working for Blake and they'd run into one another in Paris. The rest, according to Leslie's statement, was fated.

They'd confirmed that it was Leslie who had trashed Robin's trailer. Apparently, Blake had assigned her with getting the flowers in the first place. She'd gone into a jealous rage when she'd seen how much Robin had appreciated the flowers and had destroy them in a fit.

"What am I doing wrong?" She glanced over at Blake after a cloud of smoke started billowing out of the waffle iron. Blake glanced up from his computer screen and laughed at her.

"Nothing," he said. He pulled out his phone, and pointed it at her.

"Don't you..." Snap. She blew a strand of hair out of her eyes. "I'll get you for that." She turned away from him to look down at the black crust as gooey batter oozed from the center of the burned waffle.

When her cell phone rang, she hit the speaker button and answered her sister's call.

"Morning," she answered cheerfully.

"Robin!" Claire screamed into the phone. "Help us!"

Then the line went dead and the bowl of batter she'd been holding hit the ground with a plop.

The Pride Series

Finding Pride

Discovering Pride

Returning Pride

Lasting Pride

Serving Pride

Red Hot Christmas

My Sweet Valentine

Return To Me

Rescue Me

A Pride Christmas

The Secret Series

Secret Seduction

Secret Pleasure

Secret Guardian

Secret Passions

Secret Identity

Secret Sauce

Secret Obsession

Secret Desire

Secret Charm

The West Series

Loving Lauren

Taming Alex

Holding Haley

Missy's Moment

Breaking Travis

Roping Ryan

Wild Bride

Corey's Catch

Tessa's Turn

Saving Trace

Christmas Holly

The Grayton Series

Last Resort

Someday Beach

Rip Current

In Too Deep

Swept Away

High Tide

Sunset Dreams

Lucky Series

Unlucky In Love

Sweet Resolve

Best of Luck

A Little Luck

Christmas Wish

Silver Cove Series

Silver Lining

French Kiss

Happy Accident

Hidden Charm

A Silver Cove Christmas

Sweet Surrender

Second Chances

Entangled Series – Paranormal Romance

The Awakening

The Beckoning

The Ascension

The Presence

The Calling

The Chosen

Haven, Montana Series

Closer to You

Never Let Go

Holding On

Coming Home

The Hard Way

Pride Oregon Series

A Dash of Love

My Kind of Love

Season of Love

Tis the Season

Dare to Love

Where I Belong

Because of Love

A Thing Called Love

First Comes Love

Someone to Love

Wildflowers Series

Summer Nights

Summer Heat

Summer Secrets

Summer Fling

Summer's End

Summer's Wish

Distracted Series

Wake Me

Tame Me

Stand Alone Books

Twisted Rock

Hope Harbor

Raven Falls

Angel Bluff

For a complete list of books:

http://JillSanders.com

ABOUT THE AUTHOR

Jill Sanders is a New York Times, USA Today, and international bestselling author of Sweet Contemporary Romance, Romantic Suspense, Western Romance, and Paranormal Romance novels. With over 75 books in eleven series, translations into several different languages, and audiobooks there's plenty to choose from. Look for Jill's bestselling stories wherever romance books are sold or visit her at jillsanders.com

Jill comes from a large family with six siblings, including an identical twin. She was raised in the Pacific Northwest and later relocated to Colorado for college and a successful IT career before discovering her talent for writing sweet and sexy page-turners. After Colorado, she decided to move south, living in Texas and now making her home along the Emerald Coast of Florida. You will find that the settings of several of her series are inspired by her time spent living in these areas. She has two sons and off-set the testosterone in her house by adopting three furry little ladies that provide her company while she's locked in her writing cave. She enjoys heading to the beach, hiking, swimming, wine-tasting, and pickleball with her husband, and of course writing. If you have read any of her books, you may also notice that there is a love of food, especially sweets! She has been blamed for a few added pounds by her assistant, editor, and fans... donuts or pie anyone?

facebook.com/JillSandersBooks

twitter.com/JillMSanders

amazon.com/Jill-Sanders/e/B009M2NFD6?tag=jillm-com-20

bookbub.com/authors/jill-sanders

instagram.com/jillsandersauthor

www.ingramcontent.com/pod-product-compliance
Lightning Source LLC
Chambersburg PA
CBHW070938190726
48292CB00004B/1231